the Day Cometh

the Day Cometh

Total Race Separation

Jay Navies

ARCHWAY
PUBLISHING

Archway Publishing books may be ordered through booksellers or by contacting:

Archway Publishing
1663 Liberty Drive
Bloomington, IN 47403
www.archwaypublishing.com
1 (888) 242-5904

Because of the dynamic nature of the Internet, any web addresses or
links contained in this book may have changed since publication and
may no longer be valid. The views expressed in this work are solely those
of the author and do not necessarily reflect the views of the publisher,
and the publisher hereby disclaims any responsibility for them.

Any people depicted in stock imagery provided by Thinkstock are
models, and such images are being used for illustrative purposes only.
Certain stock imagery © Thinkstock.

ISBN: 978-1-4808-4820-7 (sc)
ISBN: 978-1-4808-4818-4 (hc)
ISBN: 978-1-4808-4819-1 (e)

Library of Congress Control Number: 2017910220

Print information available on the last page.

Archway Publishing rev. date: 6/26/2017

In memory of Marine Lance Corporal and Korean War veteran James H. Navies. He fought on the battlefield, seeking a better American way of life. Thank you for your service to this country. I'm proud to be your son.

12/15/26–10/11/09

Contents

Acknowledgments

I thank God for knowledge, wisdom, mercy, and grace with unlimited opportunities.

A special thanks to my mom, Joanne Navies, a very classy lady who in all ways has taught me how to love, never hate.

I especially want to thank Taj Jackson, Victoria Beeks, Tiffany Jay, and Felicia Copeland.

An honored thanks to the men and women who sacrificed their lives for justice and equality for all people.

I want to thank all my family and friends for their support. God bless.

Prologue

South Africa: The Era of Apartheid

In the dry heat of the day, Kuzemo Kenyapha, a dark-skinned African man, tethers a small goat to a partially divided fenced-in area of sheet metal shacks designating a small village. He becomes alarmed as the rickety row of houses begins to rattle and shake in front of him.

"What is happening?" screams a middle-aged African woman frantically running out of a shack, carrying her young son Zordyn Kenyapha, a half-clothed, dark-skinned small boy.

Other startled Africans rushing from their homes bear witness to white men creating thick clouds of dirt from large oil tankers and big rig trucks with huge drilling equipment as they rumble through the village.

"What are they doing here?" The African woman quickly approaches Kuzemo.

"I don't know." He wraps his arms around her and Zordyn. "But whatever it is, it doesn't look good for us."

Many Africans depart their residence and follow the vehicles.

"I must go with them." Kuzemo joins the followers.

They observe an assembly of trucks and a conference of white men standing outside a mobile office trailer.

"This land is rich!" a white man inside the trailer says to

another white man as he sprawls a fistful of sparkling diamonds and shimmering gold nuggets across the top of a desk. "And soon we'll be rich."

"Okay, but I think you're overlooking one large obstacle."

"Oh, yeah? And what could that possibly be?"

"The natives are getting restless." He points to a window, and they see a gathering crowd of Africans.

"What do they think they're doing out there?" The white man quickly swipes his valuables into a leather pouch.

"The white man has come to take all that we have!" Kuzemo shouts to a large crowd of Africans standing nearby. "They have divided our families and diluted our bloodline! And we must not allow them to do this to us! This is my son!" He lifts up Zordyn. "We must preserve our race, protect our families, and fight against them!" Those in the crowd pump their fists and loudly applaud.

"I own this land!" The white man frowns as he stares out of the window. "And there's always a solution for every situation."

Busloads of white men armed with rifles approach the Africans. They exit the vehicles and begin their merciless assault, slaughtering black people as they desperately run for their lives.

Zordyn and his mother sadly stand in front of Kuzemo Kenyapha's engraved headstone. The mother kneels down and places a single flower on top of his grave. "I say to you, Zordyn Kenyapha"—she faces her son—"become a great leader like your father, and never turn your back on your African people."

"Yes, Mama." He looks into her tearful eyes.

Chapter 1

Baltimore, Maryland: The Present Day

A "National Black Caucus" banner is displayed over a platform where Dr. Teakena Corrie, a slender, thirty-two-year-old, mahogany-colored woman standing at five foot six in a green pantsuit, with blue eyes, full lips, and a small Afro, speaks to a diverse crowd of people.

"It is always good to see such great support. But the black race has become negligent and weak. We have become so consumed with our own personal lives, education, and self-preservation that we no longer practice the concept of it taking a village to raise a child. We adults are not teaching our young people how to survive, and we are losing our youngest generation at an alarming rate."

The crowd applauds.

"Knowledge is key, and we must educate our youth. We are collectively responsible for this process and the success of our heritage. Divided, we will all fall. The black race is still not positioned as an equal in this society. This is why we all need to pull up our pants and support one another. We must have true commitment within our own culture, or we will continue to lose our youth and systematically be defeated." Teakena waves. "Thank you all for your support." She steps back.

The crowd applauds.

"We receive and appreciate those encouraging words and uplifting insight," says a dark-complexioned male activist wearing a black suit and bow tie, now stepping up. "You all can also read more on Dr. Corrie's political comments in the *All about Us* magazine and other scheduled venues around the world. Thank you, Dr. Corrie."

The crowd again applauds.

Backstage, the activist offers Teakena a business card.

"Dr. Corrie, I'd like to know if I could introduce you to our civil rights leader, Zordyn Kenyapha."

"Sure." She accepts the card. "It would be an honor and a pleasure to meet with him."

A small office building located in an inner-city neighborhood facilitates the operation of several black men and women diligently filing paperwork and answering telephones.

Zordyn Kenyapha, a bald, six-foot-seven, 245-pound, forty-five-year-old man with a chiseled dark-chocolate body underneath his long-sleeved shirt and bow tie, stands behind a desk and talks on a telephone.

"No, you need to listen! I honor what Martin Luther King, Malcolm X, and many others have done for this country, but you must have forgotten who I am! I do not operate as they have. I will meet with you once more to discuss business as I try to remain optimistic of this nation." He ends the call.

The activist approaches Zordyn with Teakena.

"Mr. Kenyapha, sir, I'd like to introduce you to Dr. Teakena Corrie. She's interested in learning more about our organization, sir."

"Welcome." Zordyn smiles and shakes hands with Teakena. "I've heard a lot about you, Dr. Corrie. What brings you to us?"

"I believe in supporting each other in order to survive, and I strongly seek the advancement of black people in any way possible."

"Yes." Zordyn nods.

"I also believe you personally care about our people, and joining forces with your organization would be a great asset to us all. Not only for myself but as a positive outreach for black people everywhere."

"Yes, I do care a very much for our people, and much help is always needed."

"My interest runs deep, and like you, sir, I am also from Africa."

"Very good. I would like to speak more with you later if I may."

"Yes, of course."

"I look forward to our next meeting, then." He graciously smiles.

The Evolving Technology logo is highly visible on top of an isolated tall building as the morning sunlight shines over the business district of Baltimore.

Zordyn, wearing a black suit and bow tie, sits at the desk of a mogul, a white man sitting behind the desk of an exclusive office with a panoramic view of the city. The mogul looks through the architectural blueprints of an undeveloped and futuristic vehicle.

"Mr. Kenyapha, are you prepared to relinquish all rights and interest of this project?"

"I'm ready to become business partners."

"No." The mogul shakes his head. "I don't need any new partners. And what you have here is just an undeveloped piece of equipment."

"Much has been taken from the black race!" Zordyn promptly stands. "Many great ideas and inventions, all stolen from us!"

"Zordyn." He sighs. "I'm offering you a lot of money for your work, enough to help you and your people."

"You care nothing about my people. I come from one of the richest lands on earth, and many of my people still live in poverty today."

"Okay. Do what you think is best." He pushes the blueprints toward Zordyn. "But you must understand. This type of technology will be developed with or without you."

"The day cometh when the black race will all rise together." Zordyn hastily collects his blueprints. "And if you care about my people, send money to Africa." He walks out of the office.

Halogen lights brightly illuminate a small garage where Zordyn stares at the metal framework of an undeveloped, ultra-modern, two-seater vehicle.

Later that evening, Zordyn, wearing his black suit and bow tie, pulls a chair out from underneath a small table in a lavish restaurant for classily dressed Teakena.

"I'm curious, Mr. Zordyn." She sits down. "Do you extend this type of hospitality to all of your associates?"

"No. But I roll out the red carpet when I see beauty and strength together."

"Oh, I see." She smiles as he sits. "So tell me. What do you have in mind for our people?"

"I seek not only to strengthen our race but technically advance our people for the future. And actually, to be quite honest, I've had my eye on you for a while now."

"I see. I'm hoping it's for something I've done well."

"Yes, of course."

"So how can I be of help to your organization?"

"I'm strongly impressed with your speaking capabilities, and I could use a woman like you to magnify my voice." He opens a bottle of wine. "I believe you and I can unify the black race in ways never done before." He pours two glasses. "Would this be of any interest to you?"

"I'm always interested in helping our people."

"Good." He gives her a glass of wine. "And with your help, I'm planning on taking black people to a whole new level." He lifts his glass.

"I'm certainly ready for that." She lifts her glass. "When do I start?"

"You already have ... by being black."

"I can definitely drink to that." She smiles, and they toast.

Chapter 2

Mary Wilks is a naturally beautiful, twenty-seven-year-old, 120-pound, olive-complexioned, shapely white woman who's about five foot four with long, sandy brown hair pulled into a ponytail. She observes several teenage students engaging in multiple activities inside various classrooms as she strolls through the hallway of a high school in her flower-printed pink dress.

Mary walks into a teacher's lounge and sees Fahleah Reese, a dark-complexioned black woman with a short Afro, relaxing on a sofa.

"Hi, Fahleah."

"Hello, Mary."

Mary walks to a vending machine, inserts money, and selects a beverage. "So what's going on in your classroom? Anything new?" She retrieves a can of soda from the machine and sits next to Fahleah.

"I see the school's curriculum has gotten a bit tougher this year, and the students are going to need to focus more."

"You're right."

"It's like these kids are more addicted to social media and less with schoolwork."

"Yeah. Some of my students have gotten so distracted I've had to take cell phones and other personal items away from them. I'm surprised some of them even make it to school on time each day."

"I'm gonna start giving out more homework. That'll keep 'em busy."

"Good idea."

They chuckle.

Eddy Haze, a six-foot-two, caramel-toned, thirty-year-old black man with short, wavy hair and a 210-pound athletic build, walks into the lounge wearing a blue suit.

"Good afternoon, ladies." He walks toward the vending machine.

"Hello," Fahleah says.

"Good afternoon, Mr. Haze," Mary responds.

Eddy inserts money into the machine and selects a beverage.

"Can I buy you ladies anything to drink?"

"No, thanks," both ladies answer.

"Is everything okay in each of your classrooms?"

"So far, so good," Fahleah says.

"I'm all good here," Mary replies.

"Okay, good." Eddy walks toward the door. "If you ladies need anything, let me know."

"I surely will," Fahleah says.

"Thanks, Mr. Haze," Mary says.

"Oh, um, Ms. Wilks"—Eddy abruptly stops in the middle of the doorway—"can I see you in my office after class today?"

"Yes, sir."

"Okay. Thanks."

Eddy walks out of the lounge.

"Girl, he is truly one fine brother," Fahleah lustfully says. "Don't you think so?"

"I guess. I mean, I never really looked at him like that."

"You saying a nice-looking, educated man like that hasn't caught your eye?"

"I've never looked at him in that way."

"I'm surprised he hasn't tried to approach any of the staff members here."

"What makes you think he hasn't already?"

"I don't think he has because I would have heard about it by now. And I haven't heard any juicy gossip on him yet."

"Well, that's good."

"Girl, I'm telling you all he gotta do is ask for my number." She mimes a phone call. "'Cause I can definitely get with him. Hello."

"I hear you." Mary takes a quick sip. "I need to get back to my classroom." She stands up and walks toward the exit.

"Yeah, I do too."

"I'll see you later."

"All right. Have a good day."

"You too." Mary leaves the room.

Mary walks into a classroom filled with a diverse group of teenagers sitting at their desks. She writes the words *future space travel* on a chalkboard, and as the bell rings, the students quickly prepare to exit.

"Okay, you all, don't forget to do your homework!" she shouts as they rush out of her classroom. "Big test on Monday. You all have a nice weekend!"

Eddy sits behind a desk in his private office and hears a knock on the door.

"Come in!"

Mary enters.

"You said you wanted to see me after class, sir."

"Yes. I have something very important I need to discuss with you."

"Okay." She walks toward him as he walks around the desk.

"Has everyone left?" He stands directly in front of her.

"There's no one here but us."

"Good."

They embrace and passionately kiss.

"Lady, I've been waiting for this kiss all day."

"I sure do hope so," she says, holding on to him. "And I've just discovered you have a secret admirer."

"Oh, really. And how do you know that?"

"I have different ways of hearing things."

"Nah." He shakes his head. "I haven't heard anything or received any flirtatious invitations from anyone."

"Well, you're wrong about that, sir. Because you definitely have one ... or two."

"If it's not you, who else could it be? Not that I'm interested, of course."

"She's the first lady of gossip around here."

"I have no idea who you're talking about."

"Fahleah Reese."

"Fahleah?"

"Yep. She likes you."

"Really?"

"Yeah."

"I never would have thought that."

"Well, it's certainly not hard to see why." She strokes his arm.

"The gossip lady, huh? So that's what she's known for around here?"

"Uh, uh-huh." Mary giggles.

"But that also lets you know how nosey she is too."

"That's true. But no one knows about us."

"Speaking of secrets, there's an old spot I wanna take you to."

"Hmm ... where are we going this time? Is it one of my favorites or somewhere new?"

"You just gotta wait and see. I'll explain everything when we get there." He quickly pecks her lips.

Later that day as daylight fades, Eddy and Mary stroll through a wooded park and stop at an old wooden bench in a partially secluded grassy area.

"Yep. This is it, Mary." Eddy nods as he surveys their surroundings. "This used to be the spot."

"It's been a long time since I've seen this place." She smiles and sits on the bench. "It was definitely one of our favorites, back in college."

"Yes, it was." He sits next to her rubbing his fingers over the weather-beaten initials "E.H. LUVS M.W." carved into the bench. Reminiscing, she also looks at the letters and suddenly laughs.

"What's so funny?"

"I remember when that park ranger almost caught you with your pants down."

"That wasn't funny, Mary." He shakes his head, smiling. "I was so scared. I still don't remember how I got my ass back in those pants so fast."

They both laugh.

"Yeah. We did have a lot of fun here."

"Yeah, we did. But I'm still wondering. How did you find the time to meet me here as much as you did? I mean, between studying and all, and I know you weren't telling your parents you were coming to see me."

"No, I would tell them that their very smart daughter was going to the library. And I would go, but I would leave early to come see you."

"Oh ... okay."

"But now I am curious to know why you have us out here."

"Well—" He directly faces her, giving her his full attention. "Mary, we've been sneaking around for a long time now, and the way I feel about you is very real." He removes a small black jewelry box from his pocket and bends down to one knee.

"Umm … Eddy. What are you doing?" She nervously starts looking around.

"Listen to me." He looks directly into her eyes. "We're always sneaking around, trying to see each other, and I can't take it anymore. I'm tired of hiding my true feelings for you." He takes a deep breath. "I love you, Mary. And I'm ready to show the whole world how much I do." He opens the jewelry box, displaying a beautiful diamond ring.

"Mary, will you …" he starts asking, and she quickly stands and looks away before he finishes the question.

"What's wrong, Mary? I thought you'd be happy."

"Eddy," she responds with her eyes full of tears and continues to look away. "You know my family won't accept this type of marriage. And what will other people think?"

"It doesn't matter what other people think or how they feel." He attempts to regain eye contact. "How you feel about this is what really matters to me." He shakes his head. "I'm sick of this clandestine relationship and this racist world we live in." He strikes the bench. "I know you love me, Mary!"

"I do love you!" She looks into his eyes. "But what if something goes wrong or something bad happens? Then what?"

"If anything bad ever happens, we'll have to cross that road together." He takes her hand. "Mary, true love is blind. Only ignorance and hate sees color. I can't promise you we won't face racism or have difficult times in our life. That's a problem I can't solve. But we can definitely show the world how much we love each other."

"When I was a little girl, I used to dream about who I would give my heart to and who I would marry. But when I met you, everything changed."

"I know your family wants what they think is best for you.

And I do too ... for the rest of our life." He stands and wipes away her tears.

"Mary, will you marry me?"

She looks at the ring and ponders as her countenance changes to a cheerful glow.

"Yes."

"Yes?"

"Yes, Eddy."

Eddy joyfully removes the ring from the box and slides it on her finger.

"I love you, Mary." He looks deeply into her eyes. "I'm going to make you the happiest wife ever."

"I love you too." She smiles, and they passionately kiss.

Eddy is dressed in a white tuxedo, and Mary wears a lovely wedding gown as they stand at a flower-laced altar in the presence of a clergyman.

"By the power of the Father, the Son, and the Holy Spirit, I now pronounce you Mr. and Mrs. Haze ... until death do you part." The clergyman's hand motions the symbol of the cross. "You may now kiss your bride."

Eddy lifts Mary's veil and kisses his wife with delight.

Chapter 3

The early morning hour shows a mixture of teenage students with book bags, backpacks, and school supplies boarding a yellow school bus on a bustling street corner.

Bobby Walker, a skinny, 140-pound, dark-skinned, teenage black male with kinky hair, rushes out of a low-income housing complex, wearing a worn-out pair of jeans and a T-shirt of the latest fashion.

"Hey! Wait up!" He runs toward the school bus, dropping a handful of books as the vehicle drives away with a load of students.

"Ah … man. I'mma be late again." He stops running as the bus travels farther away.

Dozer, a rough-looking, teenage, black male with dreadlocks and gold teeth slowly drives a new corvette through the neighborhood.

"Yo, Bobby! What's up? He stops the car in the middle of the street.

"You miss yo' bus?"

"Yeah."

"Come on, man. I'll give you a ride." Bobby hurries to the vehicle and steps inside.

"Thanks, man."

"No problem. That's what I'm here for, to help out the community."

Dozer discreetly inhales a blunt cigarette and cranks up the music. "I gotcha." He nods and drives away.

"You wanna take a hit on some of this?"

"Nah, man. I'm good."

"This that fire weed. You sure?"

"Yeah, I'm good. I just need to get to school on time."

"You like dealin' with school?

"Yeah, it's cool. You still going?"

"Nah." Dozer sneers. "It ain't got nothin' for me." He takes another hit from his blunt. "Whatcha tryin' to learn how to do anyway?"

"I wanna go to college and become an auto engineer."

"You wanna be a mechanic?"

"Nah," Bobby says and laughs. "A design engineer. That's the person who decides how the car is gonna look."

"Man, you gotta be real smart to do somethin' like that."

"I can do it. And they make big money too." He checks out the scenery. "And I can get out this hood."

"Go 'head, bruh. I hear yah. Hope you make it."

"I'm tired of being broke every day."

"Me too. That's why I gotta get this paper." Dozer drives to the front of a high school building.

"Thanks for the ride, man. I didn't think I was gonna make it today."

"It's all good. Glad I can help out."

Bobby opens the car door and partially moves out of the vehicle.

"Hold up. How yo' pockets lookin'?"

"Dude, I'm broke. I ain't got money for lunch."

"I do." Dozer smiles and pulls a fat wad of cash from his pocket.

"Damn, man! How you come up like that?"

"I can show you better than I can tell you."

The school bell rings.

"Man, I'm late again." Bobby grabs his books. Dozer skims a bill off the top of his wad.

"Here, take this with you."

"What's this for?"

"You say you broke, right?"

"Yeah. But what I need to do for this?"

"Nothin'. It's all good. Just a little somethin' so you can eat."

"Thanks." Bobby takes the money and shoves it in his pocket. "I gotta get to class, man."

"All right. Well, think about what I said and come see me later."

"Okay."

Bobby quickly exits the vehicle and runs inside the school building.

Mary stands in front of a classroom full of students.

"I hope you all had a nice weekend. Now it's time to focus on today's test."

Bobby rushes into Mary's classroom with books in one hand and the top of his sagging waistband in the other hand.

"Hold up, Mr. Walker! You're late!" Bobby stops near the door. "Tardiness will not be tolerated in my classroom. Do you understand?"

"Yes, ma'am."

"Now pull up your pants and go have a seat." Bobby tightens the grip on his waistband and walks past several snickering students before taking a seat near the back of the room.

"I want to discuss a new discovery before you all get started with your test." Mary grabs a glass cube with an orange rock mounted inside from off the top of her desk. "Scientist have discovered water on Mars, and this is a piece of that planet brought back from astronauts." She displays the object. "With advanced technology, scientists are now saying Mars may be a suitable place to live. Would any of you all like to live on Mars?"

A teenage white female raises her hand.

"Yes, Lisa?"

"I think it would be interesting to go see another planet, but I don't think I would want to live there."

"Yeah, it would definitely take some getting used to. Anyone else want to comment about Mars?" Mary looks around the room and sees Bobby's inattentiveness as he inconspicuously gazes at a one-hundred-dollar bill.

"Mr. Walker!" she shouts, startling his daydream.

"Yes, ma'am?" He quickly shoves the money back into his pocket.

"Would you please stand and give a comment about the subject we're on."

He stands and muddles, "Uh ... I agree with what Lisa said." The other students begin to laugh at him.

"Y'all know what?" He angrily grabs his books off the top of his desk. "I ain't gotta take this." He walks toward the door.

"Um ... Mr. Walker, where do you think you're going?" Mary places the Mars object on her desk. "Stop!" She quickly blocks the doorway.

"I got something I need to do."

"Well, you don't have permission to leave this classroom!"

"Ms. Wilks, I gotta go." He squeezes past Mary.

Bobby briefly looks back as he walks away from the school building.

Later that evening Mary steers a small car into the driveway of a quaint two-story home located in the center of a quiet middle-class neighborhood. She steps out of the vehicle with schoolbags and walks inside the home.

"Honey, it's me! She enters the home, dropping the bags at the front door. "Where are you?"

"I'm back here!"

Mary hears Eddy and walks into the kitchen. "Hey, babe."

"Hi, honey." Eddy stirs a pot over the stove.

"Whatcha cooking?"

"I'm trying a little something new." He shuffles closer to her. "I hope you're ready to eat."

"Sorry, babe. I'm not very hungry. But I'm glad to see you in such a good mood."

"I try to always be in a good mood." He kisses her. "Uh-oh." He notices her somber demeanor. "I know that look. What's wrong?"

"Nothing. I don't want to ruin our evening with the craziness of school."

"Tell me what happened. Did the gossip lady have something stupid to say?"

"No, but, one of my students walked out of class today."

"Really? Who was it?"

"Bobby Walker. You know who I'm talking about, don't you?"

"Yeah. He's a pretty smart kid. What happened? Did he say why he was leaving?"

"No. He walked in late this morning, and I noticed he wasn't very attentive. So I asked him to explain how he felt about today's subject, and he got up and walked out.

"That's strange."

"He did tell me he had something to do."

"Maybe he's got problems at home or something. I don't know."

"Yeah, but this is his senior year. And he might not graduate. These kids don't understand how important an education is until it's too late."

"I'm sure he'll come back."

"I hope you're right."

"Well, since you're not very hungry, how about I pour us a glass of wine so you can relax?"

"That sounds like a great idea." She gives a quick kiss and walks away. "Why don't you grab the whole bottle and meet me upstairs."

"Okay, on my way." He shuts down the stove and grabs a bottle of wine on his way out of the kitchen.

Betty Walker, a dark-complexioned, heavy-set, black woman wearing a nightgown relaxes on a sofa and watches television inside a small apartment.

"Auntie, I'mma make a quick run to the store." Bobby enters the room wearing a black hooded jacket.

"Don't you have school tomorrow?"

"Yes, ma'am."

"Well, it's a little too late to be going out."

"It's only nine o'clock. That's not late." He discreetly walks behind the sofa.

"Okay, well, you be careful. It ain't safe out there in those streets, especially for young black boys."

"Yes, ma'am." He walks out of the apartment, and his apparel goes unnoticed.

Dozer drives to the front of the apartment complex as Bobby exits the building.

"You ready to go make this money?"

"Yep." Bobby steps inside the vehicle.

"Let's get it."

He drives away.

Dozer stops at the curb of a high-traffic intersection in an urban neighborhood.

"All right, man. This the spot.

Bobby surveys the area. "Man ... I ain't never done this before."

"It's easy to do. Just give 'em what they want and take the money."

"I don't know about this." He shakes his head.

"You ain't punkin' out on me, are you?"

"Nah."

"Then go handle yo' business. And in a minute yo' pockets gonna be fat."

Bobby reluctantly opens the car door. He pulls the hoodie over his head and steps out of the vehicle.

"You rollin' with the big boys now." Dozer smirks. "I'll be back in a minute." He leaves Bobby standing on the street corner.

Moments later a car stops at the intersection, and Bobby quickly approaches the passenger's side of the vehicle. He makes a discreet hand-to-hand transaction, and the car drives away.

An advocate, a dark-skinned black man dressed in a black suit and bow tie, stands near the intersection with a handful of magazines.

After seeing Bobby's transaction, he approaches him. "Excuse me, young brother. Can I talk to you for a moment?"

"I don't know you. What's up?

"I see what you're doing out here, and that's not good."

"Man, you didn't see me do nothing." He lowers his head and hides his face.

"What you're doing is wrong, little brother. And you could get in some serious trouble out here. Young man, I've been there before, and I'm just trying to help you out."

"Well then, you know how hard life is without no money."

"I understand that too."

"Man ain't nobody tryin' to help nobody, for real." Bobby removes the hood and lifts his head. "So what you talking about?"

"I'm saying … when you bring your problems to the streets, you give up hope. I used to be out here just like you … until I met Mr. Kenyapha."

"I don't know who he is."

"Here. Take this." He offers Bobby one of the magazines.

"What is that?"

"It's the new *Wise and Rise* publication from Zordyn Kenyapha. He helped me change my life, and he can help you too. But first, you got to wanna help yourself. You hear what I'm saying."

"Yeah." He takes the magazine.

"Little brother, you got your whole life ahead of you. And you can change things. Read it. And I guarantee he'll help you too. But you need to get off this street, so you can wise and rise. Okay?"

Bobby nods and walks away from the corner.

"Wise and rise, little brother! Wise and rise to the top!" the advocate shouts as Bobby walks farther away.

Chapter 4

Ten Years Later: The Scope of Humanity

A "Welcome to the Black Expo" sign hangs over the entrance of a large convention center located in the heart of the city. While massive crowds of mostly black people flood the open building, smaller groups gather around departments with posted labels— "Electronics," "Software Development," "Mobile Apps," "Digital Media," "Inner Space Crafts," and "Outer Space Crafts."

"Hey, Mary, let's see what's going on over here." Eddy and Mary are among a smaller group of spectators casually strolling near the inner space department, and they see a young black man dressed in a black suit and bow tie representing on stage.

"Hello, everyone," a handsome Bobby Walker says, standing about six feet tall with an added twenty pounds, sporting a fresh-cut faded hairstyle. He moves in front of the small audience gathering around him.

"Welcome to the high-tech inner space department presented by Mr. Zordyn Kenyapha. My name is Bobby Walker, and I am the architectural designer of this fabulous ZKC Excel hovercraft." He points to an exotic blue, two-door, two-seater hatchback with no wheels on a viewing platform. "I will now demonstrate the operation of the ZKC Excel." Bobby begins to type on a keypad, and a three-dimensional image of the vehicle appears on a large computer screen. "Our innovative technology makes this vehicle the only hovercraft in production at this time." The image of the vehicle rotates on the computer screen. "This vehicle can be operated by remote control or by the touch of a finger." Bobby holds up a small device and aims it toward the Excel. He pushes a button, and the vehicle's lights come on, the doors open, and the hatchback lifts up. "The computer screen will demonstrate some of its advanced features." The image of the open vehicle is also displayed on the computer screen. "To activate the Excel without a remote, the operator's finger must be placed on the on-board computer screen mounted inside the dashboard of the vehicle." The computer screen shows the image of a finger being scanned on the Excel's dashboard computer.

"This finger scan will activate the vehicle's unique 4.7 jet engine. The Excel is equipped with special electromagnetic sensors to modify gravity and balance the vehicle over any surface, in any atmosphere."

The computer screen rotates the image to show the engine, and four round sensors placed underneath the vehicle.

"The Excel is also capable of reaching a top speed of three hundred miles per hour. This thing can really fly!"

"I like it." An Asian woman steps closer to Bobby. "Is it available? And where can I buy one?"

"Yes, the Excel is now available for purchase. It can be special-ordered from any one of your local car dealerships."

"Thank you." She closely inspects the vehicle.

"Again, my name is Bobby Walker, designer of this beautiful Excel manufactured by the Zordyn Kenyapha Corporation. This completes my presentation, and I hope I've answered all of your questions." The people in the crowd nod and clap as they begin to move away from the area. "Thank you all for stopping by." Bobby waves to the dissipating audience and aims the remote at the Excel. He pushes a button, and the doors close, the hatchback lowers, and the lights go out.

"Hi, Ms. Wilks!" Bobby notices Mary.

"Bobby? Is that you?"

"Yes, ma'am."

"Oh, my God!" She lifts her hands to her face. "Look at you. You're all grown up now."

"Yes, ma'am." He grins.

"I barely recognize you."

"Hey, babe, look." Marry turns Eddy. "You remember Bobby Walker? My old student?"

"Yeah. Hello, Bobby."

"Hi, Mr. Haze."

Bobby and Eddy shake hands.

"What are you guys doing together?"

"Well, we've gotten married since the last time you saw us. So I'm Mrs. Haze now."

"Oh, okay. Congratulations to both of you."

"Thank you." Eddy responds. "It's good to see you doing well for yourself."

"Yeah, I'm doing okay."

"Where did you learn how to do all of this?" Mary asks.

"I had the opportunity to meet Mr. Kenyapha. He encouraged me to go back to school and finish college. And now I work for his company."

"Congratulations to you. Now you see how important it is to have a good education."

"Yes, ma'am."

"Yeah, Mary. I remember you telling me how smart he was."

"Yep."

"Thanks for being a good teacher, Mrs. Haze. I'm just trying to do my best now."

"Well, you're welcome. And I'm very impressed."

"Thanks." Bobby smiles. "Have you all visited our outer space department?"

"No, we just got here."

"Mr. Kenyapha has also developed commercial space shuttles."

"You mean like the ones that can go to the Moon?" Eddy responds.

"Yes, sir. We'll soon be able to go to other planets as well."

"Oh, okay. Where is it?"

"It's on the other side of this building." Bobby points in that direction.

"All right, we'll go take a look."

"Okay, well, we're not going to hold you up." Mary observes a new group of spectators entering the department. "It was a pleasure seeing you again, Bobby."

"It was good seeing both of you too."

"I'm sure we'll all meet again."

"Yes, ma'am."

"Keep up the good work."

"Yes, sir. Bye, bye."

They all wave to one another as Eddy and Mary walk away.

"Hello, everyone." Bobby proudly directs his attention to the small audience gathered around him. "Welcome to the high-tech inner space department presented by Zordyn Kenyapha. My name is Bobby Walker, and I am the architectural designer of this fabulous ZKC Excel hovercraft."

The next day Mary watches television while washing dishes in her kitchen at home. She occasionally looks out the window and sees Eddy cutting grass.

A televised jingle followed by breaking news captures Mary's attention.

"Global Broadcast Network station (GBN) has interrupted

your regular scheduled programming," a white woman reports from a newsroom.

"Massive crowds of black people have all gathered together to completely saturate the Capitol Hill mall. Millions more have tuned in to our station from all over the world to hear a scheduled speech from the billionaire businessman Zordyn Kenyapha. We now take you live to one of our field reporters reporting close to the action."

A white man standing in front of a camera near an excited crowd of black people outside the Capitol speaks into a microphone.

"In just a few moments from now, Zordyn Kenyapha will stand on a stage just a few feet away from us, and he will deliver a speech to this live and vivacious audience."

The reporter moves closer to a group of black people.

"I'm here with some of the faithful supporters waiting to hear his speech and possibly catch an up-close glimpse of Mr. Kenyapha." He singles out a black woman from the group.

"Hello. I'm reporting live from GBN news. Do you know what type of message Mr. Kenyapha is going to present to us today?" The woman speaks into the microphone.

"Umm ... yeah. Mr. Kenyapha has always been a positive speaker and great role model not only for black people but all people. I'm sure he'll talk about education and politics and stuff like that. But I know whatever he has to say, it'll be inspiring and uplifting to all of us."

"Okay, thank you." The reporter looks into the camera. "I'm sure whatever Mr. Kenyapha says, these people are anticipating a powerful message from the civil rights and business leader."

Mary immediately opens the kitchen window.

"Eddy! Eddy!" She frantically waves her hand to get his attention.

Eddy sees Mary and stops the lawnmower.

"What is it?"

"Come quickly! Hurry!"

Eddy rushes into the kitchen.

"What's up?"

"Look." She points to the television. "Zordyn Kenyapha is about to give a speech.

"I knew about it."

"Well, I didn't want you to miss it."

"He ain't sayin' nothing new or talking about anything we haven't heard already."

"Zordyn Kenyapha has just walked out on stage," the field reporter says as the enormous crowd begins to cheer and clap.

Zordyn Kenyapha, dressed in a black tuxedo, stands on a platform behind a podium surrounded by microphones and cameras.

"Today is a great day!" He lifts his hands, and the audience joyfully responds. "I have great news." He lowers his hands, and the crowd becomes completely silent as he positions a microphone and steps closer to the podium.

"I first give honor to all black leaders who previously paved the way set before me. But I stand here because some of the same racial problems that have plagued our race for many years still persist to this day. This world is cruel, and the black race has always struggled. We do not seek to destroy this great nation we helped to build, but we continue to fight for justice, equality, and economic change. And yet we persevere, and we've always remained hopeful. Black people have always been used and abused throughout this land for centuries. With police brutality, terrorist attacks, and increasing violence, I don't believe we will ever be received as equals on this planet. So I'm forced to personally ask each and every one of you a serious question. And that is this. Where do you all see yourselves in the future? Under great leadership in the past, we as a people have flooded these same grounds, asking for the same thing in our quest for equality and justice time after time.

But this shall not go on any longer. Today I have a solution. I have developed a plan that will completely transform the course of our lives forever. I have begun construction of a great city on the planet Mars. This is a place where we can all live together peacefully.

"I can provide the best educational programs available with unlimited employment opportunities and lucrative benefits, free health care plans, and new home ownership for all of you. The day has come for us to ascend to the next level. And I'm asking all black people and all people considered black from all over the world to join me. Collectively, we have the resources to move forward, and I need all of you to make this journey a success. I'm offering each and every one of you access to a better life. I propose a new way of living and the perfect opportunity of a lifetime. I'm calling for total race separation from this planet. But we must examine our past before we move forward." He steps back and looks over the crowd.

"Are you all with me?" He spreads his arms, and the entire crowd erupts with a thunderous applause.

"Good!" He nods and lowers his arms to once again silence the crowd. "I have space shuttles prepared for boarding, and the transition is effective immediately."

Zordyn lifts one finger in the air and shouts, "Wise and rise," and each audience member energetically lifts a finger and chants, "Zordyn! Zordyn! Zordyn!"

"May your journey be peaceful." Zordyn steps back and looks over an extremely excited crowd.

"Okay, I think that man has just lost his mind!" Mary turns to Eddy. "You didn't know about this?"

"No!" He shakes his head. "I knew he was going to give a speech, but I don't think anybody saw that coming."

"That's no speech! That's crazy! How in the hell can an entire race just move to another planet?" She throws a dish towel into the sink.

"Damn, Mary. Calm down." He comfortingly rubs his hand across her back. "I don't think I've ever seen you so upset."

"You wanna talk about racial discrimination. He's only adding problems to the difficult race relationship we already have. And he calls himself a civil rights leader."

"Mary, relax."

"The man's an idiot, and he's only starting more trouble! I just can't believe the dumb crap I just heard." She shakes her head. "I mean ... he could be starting something very serious."

"Everything will be all right."

"Honestly, do you think anybody'll go with him?"

"I don't know. He's got a lot of followers. Somebody might go with him, but he's not going to be able to achieve complete race separation. That's impossible."

"Would you ever think about leaving?" She looks into Eddy's eyes.

"Come on, Mary. I can't believe you would ask me something like that." He raps his arms around her. "We've dealt with a lot of racial adversities. I don't see this being any bigger than anything else we've ever had to deal with. Beside all that, did you forget about our marriage vows?"

"No, I did not."

"Till death do we part, right?"

"That's right." She smiles.

"Well, don't worry about it. We'll make it through whatever happens together, okay?"

"Okay."

Chapter 5

A digital "Mars Space Shuttles Now Boarding" sign is displayed over a special boarding gate inside an airport.

A black female flight attendant in uniform stands at a designated entrance and guides a wide variety of black people with boxes, bags, and luggage through a terminal passageway.

A young black girl holding her teddy bear and a suitcase pauses near the attendant.

"Excuse me, miss. Is Mars going to be a beautiful place for all of us? Because Poof and I are very excited to go." She holds up the teddy bear.

"Aw ... she's cute."

The attendant flicks the bear's ear.

"I'm just as excited to go as you are because I haven't been to Mars yet either. So you'll get to see it before I will."

"I hope it doesn't take very long to get there."

"It should be just a few hours, and you'll be there in no time."

"Good. Because I don't wanna fall asleep and miss anything."

The attendant laughs.

"I'm sure you and Poof won't miss anything."

"Okay. Bye, bye." The girl waves and proceeds to walk through the terminal with her parents.

"Have a good flight."

Many black faces are seen through the windows of a unique

ZKC-labeled airplane-like shuttle with two wings on each side of the fuselage as it travels down a runway and lifts off into the air.

A wide variety of poorly to well-dressed Africans carrying boxes, bags, luggage, and personal items run and walk from all directions to a large ZKC space shuttle positioned for boarding in an open rural area of Africa.

An African woman walking toward the shuttle stops and removes a wicker basket from the top of her head.

"Ons almal gaan na die hemel daarbo (we all go to the heavens above)," she says in her native language. She drops to her knees. "Na'n nuwe Afrika (a new Africa)!" She lifts her hands to the sky.

Several white patrons socialize and drink as they watch television programs from multiple screens positioned around a bar located inside the center of a restaurant.

"This whole Mars thing is starting to affect the number of students we have in our school district." Eddy says to Mary while they eat at a small table near the bar.

"I know. Some of the parents are actually coming in and taking their kids right out of my classroom. Can you believe it?"

"No, I couldn't have ever imagined something like this happening in my lifetime."

"I just don't understand how this so-called transition is going to make things better for anybody. I know I certainly wouldn't want to go to a planet I knew absolutely nothing about."

"I agree. But people are doing it."

"Hey, send me a beer!" a young white woman sitting at the counter of the bar orders.

"One beer coming up!" A white male bartender pops the cap on a bottle of beer and slides the drink to her.

"Thank you." She drinks.

Eddy glances at the patrons sitting around the bar and sees a partially concealed handgun inside the young white woman's waistband.

"It does feel kinda strange knowing that black people are actually leaving this planet." He looks around the area. "I remember when this restaurant used to be full of all kinds of people. Now I see I'm the only black person in here."

"It's just different people on different days. That's all." Mary briefly looks around.

"I'm also starting to notice more people carrying concealed weapons too. I think I might need to buy me a gun."

"Stop it, Eddy. I think you're starting to overreact."

"No, I'm serious." He chuckles.

The televised jingle followed by breaking news is broadcasted on all televisions, capturing every ones attention.

"Global Broadcast Network station has interrupted your regularly scheduled programming," the white woman reports from a newsroom. "Good evening, everyone. Our top story, more African-Americans are leaving the planet than anticipated."

"Hey, hey, be quiet! I wanna hear this!" the young white woman sitting at the counter demands. "Can you turn it up?" she asks the bartender, and he increases the volume by remote control as the newsroom reporter speaks.

"Many African-Americans have come to believe that Mars may be a well-thought-out solution to their economic and racial problems. A recent worldwide poll was taken, and surprisingly, 80 percent of white Americans believe that this world would maintain its economic structure and may possibly be better off without blacks." Placing her hand over her ear, the reporter pauses a moment. "I'm receiving information of a special broadcast announcement coming from the president of the United States. We now go live to the White House."

The US president, an older, noble, white man with partially

gray hair, appears on all television screens as he sits behind an official desk.

"To Africans, African-Americans, and all people of color, for many years it has become our national goal to combat racism in America and abroad. We have eliminated slavery and implemented new laws to prevent discrimination of any kind. I regret the possibility that many of you may feel as though your lifetime struggle and commitment for equality has failed and your diligent process for justice has been denied and that you must now lead your life on another planet. America is the land of the free and the brave, and I will continue to do what is necessary for all people to prosper here in this country.

"But I must say as president of the United States, I believe all people should have the option to live wherever they so choose. And if any race believes they can achieve a greater success on Mars or abroad, then I give without hindrance my personal seal of approval. And to all my fellow Americans, I thank you for your continued support of this great and prosperous nation."

The newsroom reporter returns to the television screens. "We will most certainly keep you up to date and informed on the latest news as this racial situation develops. This has been breaking news from the Global Broadcast Network station, GBN. We now return to your regularly scheduled programming."

All of the televisions return to different programs, and the bartender lowers the volume.

"Well, it looks like our race problems just might be solved!" a big burly white guy with the words "White is right" and a confederate flag tattooed on the back of his bald head responds. "What we need niggers for anyway?" He draws everyone's attention, including Eddy's.

"What?" He throws up his hands. "Was it something I said? 'Cause I got the right to say whatever I want, don't I?"

"Yes, you certainly do." the white woman with the concealed weapon replies.

The bartender knocks the head of beer off a mug and slides the glass to the bald guy.

"Hey, buddy. This one's on the house."

"Thanks." The bald guy raises the mug. "Black people oughta be glad to be in America anyway." He chugs the beer as other customers begin to laugh. "They can never just sit down, shut up, or be quiet." He slams the mug on top of the bar. "They're always complaining."

"And I'm not about to sit down or be quiet after listening to an ignorant asshole like you!" Eddy directs immediate attention to the bald man as he stands in anger.

"If you don't like what I said, you can take matters into your own hands, or you can take your black ass to Mars. Your choice!" The man pushes away his drink and stands firm.

Mary quickly grabs Eddy's arm as he steps forward.

"No, Eddy, don't! It's not worth it."

"You know this used to be one of my favorite restaurants," he says to Mary, shaking his head after an intense standoff.

"Please, Eddy. Let's just go. We don't have to ever come back here again."

"I can see why people only take so much of this." Eddy places money on the table, keeping a close eye on the bald guy as he and Mary walk away from the table and out of the restaurant.

Chapter 6

Numerous consumers of different ethnicities shop throughout a wide variety of stores inside a large retail mall.

One of the smaller clothing stores inside the mall has a "World 'N' Fashion" sign and a "No Weapons Allowed" label placed on the glass door at the entrance.

"Hey, guys, wait up!" A teenage Hispanic female shouts to a group of other Hispanic teenagers while holding hands with her male companion as they all walk past the store's entrance.

"What's up, girl?" another female from the group asks.

"I wanna go inside this store. Come with me. I might find somethin' nice to wear for my papi." She smiles at her boyfriend.

"Oh ... I hope you find something sexy for me, mama."

"Let me go look." She releases his hand.

"Okay, we'll wait out here."

"Okay." She walks into the partially crowded store with the other female.

A teenage black female searching through merchandise sees a teenage white female concealing an article of clothing underneath her shirt.

The proprietor, an Asian woman, keeps an attentive eye on all patrons as she slowly walks past the two females.

The white female spots the black female looking at her and quickly turns away.

"You ready to buy now?" the proprietor suspiciously approaches the black female.

"Why you asking me that? Does it look like I'm ready to buy now?"

"No. No. Too many people in store. I just asking. No problem, okay?"

"Well, why don't you see if other people are ready to buy instead of always looking at black people?"

"Whatcha trying to say?" The white female frowns at the black female.

"I'm saying she needs to stop lookin' at me and check under yo' shirt! That's what I'm saying!"

"What's up?" a teenage white male asks the white female as a group of white teens approach.

"Is everything good over here?"

"No!" The white female points to the black female. "This bitch right here needs to mind her own damn business!"

"Who you calling a bitch! I will drag yo' ass out this store!"

"Hold up!" The white male slightly lifts his shirt above his waistline and reveals a pistol. "You don't want none of this."

"No, please! No trouble!" The proprietor sees the gun.

"Hey, y'all! Come here!" The black female shouts to a group of teenage black males.

"Whatcha need?" a black male asks as a group of teenage black males gather around her.

"This white boy over here told me I don't want none and showed me his shit."

"Oh, yeah?"

The black male lifts his shirt above his waistline and revealed a pistol to the white group of males.

"You punk-ass white boys had better get out of here."

"You ain't gone do shit to us."

"Y'all don't want none of this."

"Well, I guess we gonna have to help you niggas get to Mars!"
He places his hand underneath his shirt and nods to the group
of white males.

"Help us out then!" The black males all spread out. "We ready
to go!"

The white male pulls out his gun, and both groups of teens
point pistols at one another as several patrons begin to frantically
take cover and desperately rush out of the store.

"No! No! Please leave now!" The proprietor backs out of the
way and quickly moves to the rear of the store.

"Stop! No trouble!" Two Asian men carrying semiautomatic
rifles rush from the rear of the store. "Drop guns now!" They
demand, pointing weapons at each group of teens.

The Hispanic boyfriend walks to the entrance of the store and
freezes as he observes the situation.

The white male shoots the black male in the chest, and the
black teen falls to the floor, initiating a gun battle inside the store.

The Asian man shoots at the white male, and a bullet hits him
in the arm. But another projectile whizzes inches past his face and
strikes the Hispanic female in the neck.

"No!" the Hispanic male standing in the doorway cries as he
sees his girlfriend clutching her throat and falling to the floor.
"¡Que mueren cerdos Asiaticos (die, you Asian pigs)!" he declares
in his native language. Instantly, he removes two handguns from
his waistband and fires hysterically at the Asians as he walks into
the store.

The group of Hispanic teenagers pulls out guns and randomly
starts shooting as they run into the store.

Two black males emerge at the entrance of the store, shooting
back into the building, causing tremendous confusion and chaos
inside the mall.

A white man standing near the store shoots one of the black
males, killing him instantly as the other runs away.

"Freeze!" A uniformed black male security officer running to the scene sees the shooting and shoots the white man, and the white guy falls.

Three bloody Hispanics rushing out of the store encounter multiple gunshots from people of all races running toward the scene, and everyone begins to sporadically shoot everyone who doesn't match their own skin color as they all seek shelter in an all-out race war.

Hordes of people frantically fleeing the mall cautiously scramble toward their vehicles as multiple gunshots are heard on the parking lot.

A black woman running across the lot screams in agony as she's pierced in the leg and falls to the ground.

Eddy grabs Mary's hand, and they carefully exit the mall. They quickly run across the parking lot and step inside a midsize vehicle. Mary screams in horror as bullets hit their vehicle and Eddy hastily maneuvers away from the chaotic scene.

"Mary, are you okay?" Eddy pulls to the side of the road. "Did you get hit?"

"Yeah, I ... I think so."

"It doesn't look like it." He examines her shocked body. "Nah, you're okay. Just a lot of glass everywhere." He sits back and gives a sigh of relief. "I don't know what's going on with these people out here." He looks around and sees police cars, fire trucks, and ambulances with flashing lights and sirens whizzing past his vehicle. "I think we should get home." He slowly drives away.

Chapter 7

"It's been a long and crazy day out there." Eddy slides in bed. "Are you sure you're all right?" He observes Mary walking out of the bathroom in her nightgown, lethargic.

"Yeah." She slowly sits on the edge of the bed. "What's going on, Eddy?"

"I don't know."

"It seems like everybody has gotten more violent after that crazy speech."

"Maybe the anger has always been there, and this is an opportunity for everybody to express it more."

"It can't continue to go on like this. Something's got to give."

"Yeah, you're right about that."

"What do you think will happen?"

"I have no idea, Mary. But I think you should try to relax." He massages her back.

"It's seems like everybody wants to kill one another."

"Don't worry about it, okay? I'm just glad we got home safe."

"I've never seen anything like this."

"It'll be all right." He places his hand over hers. "Let's try to get some sleep. I'm tired." He moves over, and Mary turns off the nightlight.

"I love you." She snuggles close to Eddy.

"I love you too."

Moments later the silent night is interrupted by the sound of glass breaking.

"Eddy, did you hear that?" Mary immediately sits up.

"Hear what?" He awakens, still half asleep.

"That noise," she whispers. "It sounded like it came from downstairs." She notices a faint orange glow inside the bedroom and looks out of the window.

"Oh, my God! Eddy! There's a cross burning in the front yard!"

"What?" He promptly leaps from the bed and out of the room.

Eddy dashes out of the house with a fire extinguisher and swiftly extinguishes the flames from the large cross burning in the center of his lawn. He immediately tosses the extinguisher and removes a handgun from his waistband as he stands near the smoldering wood, looking around the neighborhood for suspicious people.

"Did you see anybody out there?" Mary meets Eddy inside the front door.

"No."

"Why do you have a gun? You gonna shoot somebody?"

Eddy replaces the gun inside his waistband and closes the door. He flips on a light switch, and they see pieces of broken glass and a brick on the floor.

Eddy picks up the brick and sees the words "Nigger Leave" marked on the side of it.

"Call the police."

Mary quickly goes into another room.

"The police are on the way." Mary walks into the bedroom and sees Eddy packing a suitcase. "What are you doing? Are we going somewhere?"

"No, not you. I'm leaving."

"What? No, you're not!" She violently knocks the suitcase off the bed.

"Look!" He grabs her. "You see what's going on out there, don't you? Well, I'm trying to keep you safe!"

"And you think leaving is going to keep me safe! No, Eddy!" She pulls away. "How in the hell could you possibly think that?"

"Because you're a white woman! That's how!"

"And what does that supposed to mean?"

"It means you don't understand discrimination like I do."

"You can't tell me what I understand!"

"Do you know what could happen to me ... or both of us if I was the only black man left here on Earth?"

"It doesn't matter. As long as we're together."

"I don't know what else to do, Mary."

"Whatever happened to you wanting the whole world to know how much you love me or the marriage vows to death do us part? What about that?"

"Mary, listen to me." He attempts to wrap his arms around her. "The last space shuttle leaves at midnight."

"How did you know about the last space shuttle?" She moves away. "You've been keeping track of it?"

"No, I wasn't. I was trying to go to sleep ... until this." He shows her the brick. "I'm just making a temporary move right now until things settle down."

The doorbell rings. Eddy opens the front door and sees a white male police officer.

"Did somebody call the police?"

"Yeah, my wife did."

The officer steps inside the house.

"Somebody burned a cross in my yard and threw this brick inside in the house." He gives the brick to the officer.

"What's going on out here, Officer?"

"I'm not exactly sure. But all law enforcement agencies across the nation are experiencing an abrupt increase in violence."

"Yeah, I had shots fired at me and my wife earlier today."

"Okay, well, I'll go ahead and write a report on this situation and send it in."

"Is that the only thing you can do?"

"Did you see anyone out there?"

"No."

"Then that's all I can do."

"Okay. Thanks for coming, Officer."

"I'll say this to you." The officer discreetly lowers his voice and makes direct eye contact. "You might want to consider getting something to protect yourself if you know what I mean."

"Yeah, I do."

"All right. Call us back if you need us."

"Okay, thanks for coming."

The officer walks out of the house.

Eddy closes the door and sees Mary standing in the middle of the staircase.

"Now do you see what I'm talking about?" He approaches her, and she immediately goes up the steps. "Mary, I'm coming back."

Chapter 8

Several ZKC space shuttles independently move through the darkness of outer space as they travel among the stars toward the distant planet Mars. The shuttles begin to fall into single formation as they approach the large orange sphere.

One shuttle deviates from the line and flies closely over a ZKC-labeled tall building and highway system lined with hovercraft vehicles.

The shuttle slowly passes over a wide variety of black people shopping at upscale stores and dining inside fancy restaurants. They operate unique hovercrafts and ride glide-bikes (motorcycles without wheels) as they move throughout the streets of the thriving community.

The shuttle passes over a bulldozer pushing heaps of red soil, and a crane positioning steel support beams underneath a giant spinning umbrella-like tower. The ship then lands behind a dome-shaped building.

Eddy carries two suitcases as he walks underneath a "Welcome to Alltuzor" sign hanging over an entrance inside the dome. He follows in line behind the newcomers, a small group of black people carrying boxes, bags, and luggage. They are all individually scanned as they walk inside a small corridor.

Eddy and the newcomers enter a huge auditorium, joining a

larger group of black people standing in front of a stage, luggage in tow.

Eddy sees two dark-complexioned black men wearing special ZKC uniforms standing nearby. The uniform is composed of a black cloth. It's a two-piece pantsuit with a green V-pattern on the front of the zip-up jacket. The jacket also has a one-inch green collar with a green clip-on badge.

"Welcome." One of the uniformed men smiles as he ushers Eddy and the newcomers farther into the auditorium.

Teakena walks to the center of the stage, wearing a tailored ZKC uniform with a skirt, high heels, and green clip-on badge.

"Hello, everybody. My name is Teakena Corrie. I'm Zordyn Kenyapha's personal assistant and your host. And we would like to welcome you all to Alltuzor, Mars. Our wonderful city is still under construction and growing as you all may have seen on your flight coming in. And that large umbrella-like structure is called a centrifuge tower. They are scientifically positioned on the planet to create artificial gravity and simulate the atmosphere of Earth. The shaft also heats the ice below the surface to produce more water and oxygen. And because the air is thinner, you all will need to receive a small pill to help the human respiratory system adapt." She holds up a small yellow pill. "This pill will serve as an adaptive hormone and necessary antibody so that each one of you can achieve optimal life expectancy in this new environment. There will also be multiple orientation classes and special health monitoring to educate you during this process. So please feel free to stop any one of our executives wearing the ZKC uniforms for any assistance or personal needs." She points in the direction of the black men wearing the uniforms. "Or anyone of you can come to my office for further assistance at any time. We hope you all had a pleasant flight to your new planet and your new home. We're all family here. So be friendly, and get to know your neighbors."

Bobby walks into the entrance of the auditorium dressed in a ZKC uniform.

"Again, my name is Teakena Corrie, and we believe all of your dreams and personal expectations will be fulfilled here on Mars."

"Hey, Eddy." Bobby sees Eddy as he walks farther into the area.

"Hi, Bobby." They shake hands. "I'm sure glad to see somebody I know because I don't know what to do next."

"Anybody can help you, but it's all good. I got you." He takes one of Eddy's suitcases. "Come on. You can come stay with me until you get your own place."

Eddy grabs the other suitcase and follows Bobby through a side door of the auditorium.

"Did you have a good flight?"

They walk inside a covered parking lot.

"It wasn't bad. It was a lot quicker than I thought it would be, but I still don't believe I'm here."

Eddy follows Bobby to a blue ZKC Excel hovering over a parking spot.

"Isn't this the vehicle you designed on Earth?"

"Yep, the same one."

Bobby points a small remote toward the vehicle, and the hatchback automatically lifts up. "I can help you get one and a good job too." He lays the suitcases in back, and they step inside the vehicle.

Bobby places his finger on a computer screen mounted inside the dashboard. His fingerprint is laser-scanned, activating the Excel and it slowly moves away from the parking lot.

The Excel moves past large contemporary homes as it glides over the street of a suburban neighborhood.

"This is where I live." Bobby points and stops near the curb of a two-story home with large steel beams and oversized glass windows.

"You like it?"

"It's nice, but I can see straight through it."

"Yeah," Bobby says and laughs. "But these houses are totally different from the ones on Earth." He aims a small remote toward the house. "Watch this." He presses a red button and the large glass sections instantly darken.

"Okay, that looks much better. Did you design that too?"

"Nah, just more black people showing off their talent."

Eddy sees another exquisitely designed three-story home sliding into position just a few feet away from Bobby's home.

"What going on with that house over there?" He points.

"This area of Mars is called 'The Ever-Changing Community' because all the houses sit on a steel grid and they can be moved at any time. So if you don't like your neighbors, you can easily slide your home to another location."

"Well, that's creative."

"Yeah, it's cool. Come on. Let's go inside."

The Excel doors open, and they step outside. Bobby removes the two suitcases from the hatchback, and the vehicle automatically closes. They step onto a conveyor belt, and it transports them to the front door of Bobby's home.

They enter the home, and Bobby places the suitcases off to the side as Eddy steps farther inside the spacious room with contemporary décor.

"This is very nice, Bobby."

"Thanks. You'll have one too. Just as soon as you get situated."

"Situated? I just left everything I know and love back on Earth. So that's gonna be kinda hard for me to do.

"I know how you feel."

"Nah, I don't think following one man to Mars was a good idea."

"Maybe not, but I don't see nothing wrong with giving it a try. I mean, what other choice did we have?"

"We can't solve a problem by running away from it."

"Yeah, but our ancestors have been dealing with racism for all their lives, and I don't wanna have to deal with that problem for the rest of my life. And I'm younger than you."

"You're right. Racism has always been a problem, and I'm not sure it will ever end. But I'm still willing to fight against it."

"Me too. But I think Mr. Kenyapha is trying to create the ultimate solution for us. "Just look at this house." He raises his hands as he steps farther into the home. "We got the best of everything right here."

"Yeah, but I really don't see this move being good for all of us."

"You'll be all right. And I'll help you with everything."

"Yeah."

Eddy stands despondent.

"Well, you're here now. Come on." Bobby motions with his hand. "Let me finish showing you around."

They walk into the kitchen.

"I named the house Serran. So it would know when I'm talking to it."

"You named your house?"

"Yeah, and it can do a lot of things just by speaking to it."

"You couldn't just say, 'House,' or is that some kinda special Mars code you need?"

"Nah." He laughs. "It's nothing special. I just like rap music, so I called it Serran. It's like a metaphor for plastic wrap. You get it? Rap?"

"No, I don't. Probably because I don't listen to that type of music."

"Well, anyway, you can still ask the house for whatever you like. You can say anything." He raises his voice. "Serran, what's the weather outside?"

"Today's forecast is sunny with a high temperature of 123 units," an automated voice responds.

"Or watch this." He moves to a marble countertop island with a gold octagon inlay. "Serran, I want two glasses of nonalcoholic Mars Red."

Two glasses full of red liquid magically rise from the center of the octagon.

"Here, taste this."

"What is it?"

"It's juice from Mars. It's like fruit punch, only better."

Eddy sips on the liquid.

"You like it?"

"Yeah, it's not bad."

"I told you."

They drink.

"You can order any kind of drink you can think of from right here."

"Okay. That's a pretty cool invention."

Bobby again motions. "Come on. I'm not finished yet. I got something I know you'll appreciate seeing." Bobby leads Eddy out of the kitchen and into the game room.

"What? You've got an old pool table? Here on Mars?!" Eddy says, walking farther into the room.

"Yep, I knew you'd be surprised." Bobby laughs. "But can you play?" Bobby sits his drink down and removes one of the pool cues from a shelf.

"I can beat you."

"Let me see what you've got."

"Okay." Eddy sits his drink down and grabs a pool cue.

"Now the game is still the same. But the rules have changed here on Mars. Instead of using the white ball to knock all the other balls off the table, we use the black ball to do it." Bobby Holds up the black ball. "This is the new cue ball."

"Okay. It doesn't matter what color the ball is, I still have the knowledge and experience to teach you a good old-fashioned lesson."

"Yeah, okay. You say that now."

Bobby racks the balls.

Eddy spots the cue ball and carefully takes aim with his stick. He skillfully strikes the black ball, knocking several other balls into several different pockets of the table.

"Okay, that was a good break."

"You ain't seen nothin' yet." Eddy carefully aims his stick toward the cue ball. "I've got the balls with the stripes."

Bobby and Eddy continue hitting assigned balls into designated pockets for a while. At the conclusion of their last game, the cue ball travels toward the white ball and knocks it into a side pocket, leaving only the black ball to freely roll over the top of the pool table.

"Well, son." Eddy celebrates. "I told you that you wouldn't beat an old pro at this game." He lays his stick on top of the pool table.

"Yeah, you got me this time, old dude."

"Ah ... okay. I gotta be called an old dude now."

"Well, I got to have something to say."

A rhythmic chime sounds.

"What's that?"

"That's my doorbell. My girlfriend and her mother were stopping by."

"Well, I need to go somewhere."

"Whatcha mean?"

"I don't want to get in your way."

"No, I want you to meet 'em. I'm sure they would like to meet you."

"No, Bobby. If you wanna see your girl, that's fine. But I'm not up for meeting anybody right now."

"Yeah, I know things are moving kinda fast for you right now, but I don't think it's a good idea for you to be hiding out either."

"I'm not trying to hide or be antisocial." He shakes his head. "I'm just not ready for all this."

"I understand." Bobby returns his pool stick to the rack. "This is new for all of us too." He walks to the door. "They're just good people trying to be friendly. That's all. But you can meet them whenever you're ready." He walks out of the room.

Chapter 9

Bobby opens the front door of his home and sees two very attractive ladies—Jessica Crystal, a petite, medium-complexioned young adult, and her mother, Delores Crystal, a voluptuous, medium-complexioned, middle-aged black woman.

"What's up, Jessy?"

"Hey."

"Hi, Ms. Crystal."

"Hello, Bobby."

"Please make yourself comfortable, Ms. Crystal. I don't ever have to say that to her," he comments as Jessica leads the way farther into the home.

"Hey! I don't hear you complaining about it." They laugh as she playfully punches his arm.

"Why do you have your suitcases here?" Jessica looks down. "You going somewhere?"

"No, those belong to friend."

"Your friend had better not be another woman."

"*He* is one of the new arrivals, and he's staying with me for a while."

"Well, where is he?"

"He's in the game room."

"How old is he?" Delores inquires.

"Um … I don't know. If I had to guess, I would say you two are probably about the same age."

"Well, I would like to have the opportunity to welcome him to Mars."

"Yeah, but he's having a little bit of a hard time taking all of this in right now."

"Oh, okay." She nods. "Is he all right?"

"Yeah, he's okay."

"Uh, um." Eddy gestures as he steps behind Bobby.

"Hey, hey!" Bobby responds. "Here he is now." He steps aside. "Ladies, I would like to introduce Mr. Eddy Haze."

"Hi, I'm Jessica."

"Nice to meet you, Jessica."

"You too, sir."

They briefly shake hands.

"And this is her mom, Ms. Crystal," Bobby says, and she steps closer.

"Welcome to Mars."

"Thanks."

"It's a pleasure to meet you."

"It's nice meeting you too, Ms. Crystal."

They cordially shake hands.

"I would prefer you to call me Delores."

"All right, I will." He nods. "Just Eddy works for me as well."

"Okay, Eddy." She gives a warm and friendly smile.

Jessica grabs Bobby's hand.

"Mom, we'll be in the backyard if you need us."

"All right, that sounds good. I think Eddy and I will be okay here." She glances at Eddy.

"Okay." Jessica walks away with Bobby.

Delores and Eddy move farther into the living room.

"Well, I know you just got here, but how do you like Mars so far?"

"It's nice from what I've seen. It looks like a lot of positive things are going on, especially with the new technology and all. But I don't know why black people couldn't do all this kind of stuff on Earth. Why did we have to come to Mars to do this?"

"I think most people would blame it all on racism, but others did it for economic reasons as well. That's why I'm here."

"Are you satisfied with that decision?"

"Yeah, I'm doing okay here."

"Well, that's good for you, but I still don't think it was a good move for all of us."

"Maybe not. But we're all here now."

"Yeah, and I guess nobody really cares about how all of this is going to affect Earth."

"I don't know, Eddy. I mean … I never really thought much about it. But I can say that if this all fails, we won't have anyone to blame but ourselves."

"Yeah, I guess so."

"Why did you come to Mars?"

"That's a good question, Delores." He slightly frowns. "I really don't know why."

"Speaking of something good." She abruptly claps, noticing his demeanor. "Have you tasted the new Mars red drink?"

"Yeah, I had some earlier with Bobby."

"Oh, okay. Well, would you mind having a glass with me?"

"Yeah, sure."

"Okay, come with me." She starts walking away. "I'll get it for us."

Eddy follows her into the kitchen.

Delores goes to the marble countertop with the gold octagon.

"House, ordering two Mars reds with 40 percent alcohol," she discreetly calls with her back turned to Eddy. "I would like to be someone you can call a good friend." She gives Eddy one of two glasses sitting on top of the counter.

"Thank you." He takes the glass. "I appreciate that."

"Yes, of course. We gotta be friendly in order to make this thing work." She lifts up her glass.

"Yeah, I guess you're right about that." He vaguely smiles, lifting his glass, and they drink.

Bobby comfortably positions himself inside an outdoor Jacuzzi as Jessica approaches with a large towel-wrapped around her body.

"Do you think your mother will like Eddy?"

"I don't know. He looks nice, and she is single. I guess it depends on what kind of person he is."

"That's cool." He nods. "Maybe she can help him get jump-started."

"I don't know why it's so hard for him? I fell in love with Mars as soon as I got here."

"Yeah, I did too. And I'm trying to seize every available opportunity I can."

"Me too." She removes her towel, revealing an appealing two-piece bikini.

"You look nice."

"You like it?" She shows off.

"I sure do like … you." He gazes at her thinly supported cantaloupe-sized breast.

"I like you too." Sliding into the water, she giggles.

"Yeah, I think black people will finally be all right this time." He reclines.

"Yeah, I do too." She snuggles under his arm.

"But you know, I was just sittin' here, thinking, and I got a question for you."

"What's up?"

"Can you tell me one thing you miss from Earth that you don't have here?"

"Ah … I don't know." She ponders. "I got everything I want right here."

"Yeah, I know. But if you had to pick something, what would it be?"

"I don't know." She sits up. "What made you think about that? Is this a trick question or something?"

"Naw, I'm serious. It's just somethin' I'm curious about, and I wanted to know what you come up with. That's all."

"Okay. And you said it's gotta be something we don't have here, right?"

"Yep."

"Well … if I had to say it, it would be white people."

"What?"

"Yeah!" She nods.

"What made you come up with something like that?"

"Because I left some pretty cool white friends back on Earth. Some Asians and Hispanics too. And you asked me what I missed, didn't you?"

"Yeah, okay." He nods. "That was a good answer. I had to leave some cool friends too. It would've been nice if all of us could have peacefully lived together like this."

"Yeah, maybe one day we can."

"Well, I ain't trying to sound all racist or nothin', but if they were all here, Mars would be just like Earth. And growing up, I didn't have much of anything. But now Mr. Kenyapha has provided us with the best of everything."

"Yeah, he definitely provided a nice city."

"Yep. He was looking out for us. And not to mention, race relations weren't gettin' any better when I left Earth either."

"I know, right. It was getting too crazy for me as well." She lays back. "And now we're here on Mars." She looks up at the stars. "Can you believe that?"

Meanwhile, partially intoxicated, Eddy sits on a sofa with less than half a glass of red juice and alcohol.

"Do you work for Zordyn?"

"Yes, I do." Delores sits nearby, sipping on her drink. "Do you have any ideas about what you'd like to do here?"

"Nah, I really don't know what I'm planning on doing right now." He finishes his drink. "That drink tasted a little different from the one Bobby gave me." He rubs his forehead.

"You okay?"

"Yeah, I'm just feeling a little light-headed." He places the empty glass on a table. "I may just be getting tired. I did have had a long day."

"Yeah, you're probably right. I'll keep my eyes on you." She gulps her drink and sits the empty glass down. "I'm enjoying your company." She moves to the sofa. "And I'm hoping you and I can spend a lot more time together." She sits close to Eddy.

"Delores." He looks directly into her eyes. "I can't deny that you are a very attractive woman, and I would love to have had that opportunity, if I wasn't married."

"Married? What?" She quickly moves away.

"Yeah, I am."

"Where is she?" Delores looks around. "Is she here with you?"

"Unfortunately, discrimination works in both ways, and she wasn't welcomed here on Mars."

"Oh, okay. I see. Well, I meant no harm to you or your wife, and I apologize for my behavior."

"You don't need to apologies. You didn't know." He stands up. "But I think I need to be alone for a while if it's okay with you."

"Yes, I understand."

"It was a pleasure meeting you, Delores."

"The same here, Eddy."

He walks out of the room.

Bobby knocks on a bedroom door in the middle of the night.

"Come in," Eddy responds.

He slowly opens the door and sees Eddy lying across the top of a bed.

"You okay?"

"No, I'm not. I'm still here."

"Delores told me what happened."

"Are they still here?"

"Nah, they left a little while ago. But can I talk to you for a moment?"

"Yeah." He sits up. "But before you say anything, I need to tell you I can't stay here and I need to go back home."

"What? No. This is your home."

"No, I made a mistake, and I should've never come here."

"Nah, Eddy. I don't think you understand. You can't go back."

"What do you mean I can't go back?" He immediately stands up.

"No, you can't! Didn't you know that before you came here?"

"No, I didn't! If I'd known that, I never would have done it! And now you're telling me I'm being held hostage?"

"No, we're not hostages. But I thought you knew you couldn't leave before you came here."

"No, I didn't."

"Look, all I know is Mr. Kenyapha made all the arrangements and spent a lot of money. And he feels like those who didn't want to come should have stayed on Earth."

"So now you're saying my life on Earth with my wife is ruined?" He falls back on top of the bed. "I made the biggest mistake of my life, and I just don't understand how running away can be good for anybody?" He begins to sob as Bobby stares. "It was stupid for me to leave Mary." He continues to cry.

"Do you have 'Perfect View' programmed on your computer at home on Earth?"

"Yeah, why?"

Bobby opens a drawer on a nightstand and takes out a remote keypad.

"I'm not allowed to do this." He sits on the edge of the bed. "But I'm gonna show you something."

He sits the keypad on Eddy's lap and aims it to an empty area of the room. "Now this will work for only a few minutes." Bobby types a sequence of letters and numbers as Eddy attentively looks on. "But if we get caught doing this, we could go to jail."

A blue holographic screen suddenly appears in front of them, and they hear a telephone dial tone.

"Now type in your telephone number at home, and the computer will instruct your wife to go online."

Eddy quickly types his number and hears a ringing telephone. Moments later the ringing stops, and the blue screen forms to a lifelike holographic image of Mary.

"Mary!" Eddy immediately stands up. "Can you see me? Can you hear me?" He moves in front of the image.

"The computer is shining a light on me, but I can see you!"

"You look so real." He stares at her image.

"Eddy, where are you?"

"I'm here with Bobby right now. But listen, I only have a few seconds to talk. Are you okay?"

"Yeah, I'm okay. But everybody's moving away from each other now that you all are gone."

"What do you mean? Are other people leaving Earth too?"

"No, they're still here. But they're starting to cling more to their own racial identity now. And rich white people are separating themselves away from everybody else."

"Wow! That's crazy!"

"Yeah, it's starting to look weird around here. When are you coming home?"

"I'm not exactly sure right now, but I'll be back soon."

"This is not good, Eddy." She sighs. "I need you." She begins to cry.

"I know, Mary. Don't cry." He reaches out, and his hand goes through her image.

"Hey." Bobby motions for Eddy's attention. "We need to disconnect this call now."

"Mary, I have to go now. But I need you to be strong right now for both of us. Okay?"

"Yeah."

"I love you. And I'll be there soon."

"Okay. I love you too."

Bobby quickly pushes a button on the keypad, and the holographic image disappears.

Eddy returns to the edge of the bed and sadly drops his head as Bobby takes the keypad and quietly leaves the room.

A dark-complexioned security guard walks through a narrow passageway and approaches a stainless steel door with an electronic touch pad. He places his hand over the touch pad. His palm is scanned, and the door slides open.

The security guard steps inside a brightly illuminated chamber and stands in front of an upright cylinder-shaped white pod. The door on the pod lifts opens, and Zordyn Kenyapha steps out, wearing a pair of white silk pajamas.

"Mr. Kenyapha, sir." The guard bows. "I apologize for disturbing your rest, but the code TDJ6 has just been violated, sir."

"What?" Zordyn frowns. "Who defies my law?"

"The transmission was terminated before we could get a lock on its location, sir."

"Find out where it came from! And don't come back until you do!"

"Yes, sir!" The guard nods and quickly leaves the chamber.

Zordyn clutches his fist and scowls.

Chapter 10

Early the next morning, Bobby wears his ZKC uniform as he stands in front of the countertop island, sipping on a cup of coffee.

"Good morning," he says to Eddy as he walks into the kitchen wearing the same clothes from the previous night.

"Good morning."

"You feeling any better?"

"Nah, not really. But I do have a question for you."

"Okay. What's up?"

"Is there any way I could talk to Zordyn?"

"I'll be helping out on a new project at work, so I'll be gone for a few days. But I can set up a job interview for you with Tekena, his secretary. You might be able to talk to him then. You wanna try that?"

"Yeah."

"All right, well, I need to go. Call me if you need me."

"Okay, thanks."

"Yep, I'll see you later."

Bobby walks out of the house.

Inside his Excel, Bobby follows behind a variety of other vehicles slowly moving on a busy highway.

Two police officers riding glide-cycles with flashing lights quickly pass between vehicles as traffic comes to a standstill.

Bobby hears a *ding* followed by an automated voice inside

his vehicle. "Traffic update. Major delays because of congestion ahead. Please use the alternate route."

Additional ground plates begin to turn over, constructing an alternative route to the city of Alltuzor.

Bobby maneuvers out of traffic and quickly travels on the newly developed highway.

Eddy enters a large atrium of the executive building, wearing a traditional suit and tie. He passes a variety of other professionally dressed black men and women wearing red or green badges as he walks toward the receptionist desk.

"Good morning, Mr. Haze." He's greeted by Delores sitting behind the desk, wearing a red badge.

"Good morning."

"How can I help you today?"

"I'm looking for Ms. Corrie's office."

"Yeah, okay. Take one of these elevators to the twelfth floor." She points. "And you'll see her office on your right."

"Okay. Thanks."

"Yeah, I'll let her know you're coming."

"All right. It's good to see you again."

"You too. Have a good day."

"Thanks." He walks away.

Eddy exits an elevator and knocks on Teakena Corrie's office door.

"Come in," Teakena responds.

He enters the office and meets Teakena standing behind her desk.

"You must be Mr. Eddy Haze?"

"Yes, ma'am."

"Good morning."

"Good morning."

They shake hands.

"Please have a seat." She sits, and he sits near her desk. "How can I assist you?"

"I'm inquiring about your employment position P-5846."

"Well, let me take a look at it." She scrolls down on an electronic tablet. "Did you say P-5846?"

"Yes, ma'am."

"Um … okay." She continues to scroll, periodically glancing up at Eddy. "I apologize, but unfortunately, that position is unavailable."

"Okay, but I was informed that that particular position was available."

"Who told you that?"

"Bobby Walker, one of your executives."

"Bobby." She ponders. "Yeah, well, that position isn't available. But I do have a list of other opportunities you are more than welcome to apply for if you're interested."

"Yeah, sure."

"Do you have your com link with you?"

"Yes." He removes a small electronic tablet from his pocket.

Teakena swipes the face of her device, and a holographic data page sticks to her finger. Eddy holds up his tablet, and she transfers the page image into his device.

"Okay, you've got it. Is there anything else I can do for you, Mr. Haze?"

"Uh … yeah. Is it possible for me to speak to Mr. Kenyapha?"

"No, I'm sorry. He's unavailable. But if there's anything you need, I'm more than happy to assist you."

"Nah, this is good enough." He holds up his table. "I'll take a look at your list and get back to. Thank you."

"You're quite welcome." She stands up. "And I'll be able to get you started as soon as possible."

"All right. Thanks for your time."

"My pleasure."

He leaves the office.

Chapter 11

Eddy enters Bobby's home. He removes his suit coat, loosens his tie, and releases an exhausting breath of air as he falls back on the sofa. He looks around and sees the remote keypad sitting on the table. He places it on his lap and hesitantly begins to type letters and numbers.

The blue holographic screen appears, and he hears the dial tone within seconds. The screen forms a grainy, unclear image of Mary.

"Eddy! Is that you? Are you there?"

"Yes, Mary! I'm here!" He stands up. "But something must be wrong because I can barely see you."

"Yeah, I can't see you either! Are you all right?!"

"Yeah, are you?"

"No, Eddy! Everything has gone terribly wrong!"

"What's going on now?"

"All the rich whites have built a new city for themselves, and all others have completely abandoned this country. And we're losing everything, Eddy. The house, the car, and everything!" She immediately starts crying. "And I've even lost you, Eddy."

"No, Mary! Don't say that! I know we're going through something unimaginable right now, and I made a big mistake by coming here, but I need you to hold on to the love we still have for each other."

"I can't do this by myself, Eddy."

"I'm coming back real soon."

"When? When are you coming?"

"Just as soon as I can. I promise."

"Eddy, I'm scared."

Two dark-complexioned policemen crash through the front door. "Freeze!" They point laser assault rifles at Eddy.

"Eddy, what's going on?"

The officer sees the holographic image of Mary.

"You are in violation of Code TDJ6!" He grabs the keypad away from Eddy.

"No, wait! Please, Officer!" Eddy pleads as the officer violently smashes the keypad to the ground, and the image of Mary disappears.

"Don't move!" The officer sneers. "You're under arrest." He handcuffs Eddy.

Eddy wears a bright yellow jumpsuit as he stands in a prison cell highly populated with medium to very light-complexioned black men all dressed the same.

A very light-complexioned young black man with hazel eyes and curly blonde hair approaches Eddy.

"Hi, I'm Geno." He extends a hand.

"Hey, I'm Eddy."

They shake hands.

"What'd they get you for?"

"I'm not sure. They said I was in violation of some kind of TDJ code or something."

"Oh, yeah!" Geno nods. "Transmitting satellite signals. That'll get you every time."

"Okay, so what does that mean?"

"That means you made a computer phone call back to Earth. And that's against the law here on Mars?"

"Well, what was wrong with doing that?"

"It's wrong because Zordyn Kenyapha is an evil prejudice dictator. That's why."

"What? Okay, wait. I don't know what you're talking about. I thought he was the one trying to help everybody."

"No ... you see how light I am." He raises his arm as a display. "My mother is black, but my father is white. That's why I look so white. And on Earth I would be considered black.

"But here on Mars, my skin color reminds Zordyn of white people. So I'm what he calls a 'consider-it.' That means he considers me white. And the lighter you are, the whiter you are to him."

"So you're saying he's using reverse discrimination on everybody?"

"That's exactly what he's doing. And he's making us all second-class citizens too."

"But why would he do that? I don't understand."

"Because he can. And I got locked up for protesting against him."

"Wait. All this sounds crazy to me."

Geno observers Eddy's frustration.

"How is he able to do all of that?"

"Have you ever been inside Zordyn's executive building?"

"Yeah."

"Did you notice all the light-skinned people wearing red badges and all the dark-skinned people wearing the green ones or collars? Just think about it."

Eddy ponders a moment as he mentally walks past other professionally dressed light-skinned people wearing red badges and dark-skinned people wearing green badges. He recalls seeing Delores at the desk with a red badge, Teakena in her office with a green badge, and Bobby in the kitchen with a green collar. "Yeah, I do remember seeing that."

"Okay. That's because red badges come with restrictions and the green badges have the authority."

"So that's what Zordyn's doing?"

"Yep. Just because people are the same race doesn't mean they'll be treated fair and equal."

"And to think, we all followed that man without knowing what kind of person he really is."

"We sure did. All of us did."

"So what's gonna happen now?"

"I don't know. That's a good question. I guess we're all stuck inside of Zordyn's sick fantasy."

"There ain't nothin' we can do to stop him?"

"How? He controls everything here."

"It's got to be a way."

"I don't think so."

Eddy grabs the cell bars and lowers his head.

"Welcome to Mars."

Geno walks away.

Several medium-complexioned male laborers wearing hard hats and red badges watch the welding operation of two large robotic arms attached to a partially finished building high above ground.

Bobby maneuvers his vehicle around the construction site and parks near the workers.

"Good morning, Mr. Walker." A laborer approaches Bobby as he steps out of his vehicle.

"Good morning. How is it going?"

"Everything is ahead of schedule and almost complete, sir."

"Very good. Mr. Kenyapha will be pleased."

"Thank you, sir."

Bobby steps forward, inspecting the robotic performance.

A police car and tow truck enters the area immediately. The tow truck slides a metal slab underneath Bobby's vehicle.

"Hey! Hey! Stop!" Bobby quickly approaches the tow truck driver. "What are you doing?"

"Mr. Walker!" The dark-skinned officer abruptly intervenes.

"What's the problem, Officer?"

"I've been instructed to confiscate your vehicle and escort you to Ms. Corrie's office."

The tow truck quickly hovers away with Bobby's vehicle.

"Yeah, I need to find out what's going on." He steps into the back of the patrol car.

Bobby walks inside Teakena's office. "Uh ... Ms. Corrie, what's going on?" He stands in front of her desk. "Why was I pulled off the project?"

"I'm sure you already know why." She frowns as she stands. "Who is Eddy Haze?"

"He's a friend staying at my house."

"Yeah, I thought so."

"Okay, so what does he have to do with this?"

"Well, your friend contacted Earth from your house today. Do you know anything about that?"

"No, I don't! And I have no idea what you're talking about either!"

"Let me put it to you like this." She leans over her desk.

"The only way he could have known how to transmit a signal was if you authorized a pass code."

"I didn't authorize anything!"

"Okay." She sits back in her chair. "Well, your friend will be imprisoned for one year, and I'm asking for your demotion."

"A demotion? Nah, I need to talk to Zordyn."

"Yeah, okay. Go ahead. Because he preferred your resignation."

"What?" He steps back. "A resignation?"

"You know how he feels about this. And I'm the one trying to help you out."

"Yeah, I'm sure."

"Well, I'll take that badge from you now." She opens her hand, and he tosses it on her desk before walking out of the office.

Teakena takes the badge, leans back, and pitches it into a wastebasket.

Chapter 12

Earth: One Year Later

The United States of America is now completely occupied by Caucasians.

Mary observes a white female real estate agent staking a "For Sale" sign in the front yard of her home from the backseat of a taxicab.

"Where to, ma'am?"

"Can you take me to the Lifetime Center?"

"Yeah, sure." The white male taxi driver nods as he slowly drives past several homes within this residential neighborhood, most up for sale.

The taxicab maneuvers around several damaged and deserted vehicles as it moves through the dilapidated community.

"Just look at this city." Mary shakes her head, observing an "Asian Hair and Manicured Nails" sign on an abandoned building and a hanging "Casa Taco" sign on another boarded-up building. "Who would've thought racism and hate would go this far and create so much damage."

"I don't know, lady. Nobody could have predicted this, and it's gotten even harder for me to make a living out here."

"It's bad for all of us now."

"Well, except for the rich people living in that big city behind the wall."

The taxi driver pulls in front of the Lifetime Homeless Center. Several white male vagrants smoke and loiter outside the large building.

"Here we are, ma'am." He retrieves her suitcase from the trunk. "You be careful out here."

"Thank you." She takes the suitcase and enters the building as the taxi drives away.

"Hello." Mary is greeted by an older white female volunteer standing behind a large counter.

"Hi."

"Do you want to stay with us?"

"Yes."

"Okay, great. My name is Sarah, and I'll need you to fill out this form for me please." She gives Mary an application and a pen on a clipboard. "And we can get you in right away."

"Thank you."

Mary completes the form and returns the clipboard to the volunteer.

"All finished?" She looks over the application and Mary's luggage. "Is this all you have?"

"Yes."

"Okay." She gives Mary a room key. "You can have room 118. It's just down this hallway." She points. "And if there's anything else you need, just let us know."

"Okay." Mary picks up her suitcase and starts walking down the hall.

"Oh! And dinner will be served in one hour from now if you're hungry."

"Okay. Thanks." She goes into her room.

A variety of poorly dressed white people stand in line at a counter, waiting for some food. As the line moves forward, Mary places her tray on top of the counter. She receives a small portion of freshly prepared food and sits at a table with many other less fortunate diners.

Mary observes other people eating around her and pushes away her tray.

"Hey, young lady, aren't you gonna eat that?" an older white man sitting nearby says.

"No. You want it?"

"Heck yeah, I want it. We're lucky to have this food."

"It's all yours." She slides the tray of food to him and walks out of the dining room.

"Are you leaving?" Sarah, the volunteer, spots Mary walking toward the front door.

"Yeah. Is it okay?"

"Oh, I wouldn't leave the protection of the shelter after dark."

"I know, but I have to go."

"Well, be careful out there."

"I will."

Mary walks out of the building.

As night falls, Mary cautiously walks along the sidewalk of a blighted community. She approaches an abandon commercial building and hears the sound of breaking glass.

"Is anybody out here?" She apprehensively moves forward, hearing more noise. "Is anybody in there?"

A scruffy gang of white teenage males with baseball bats exit the building and surround Mary.

"Hey, fellas, look who's not afraid to walk the streets at night." A white male thug excites the gang.

"Move out of my way!" Mary attempts to move in a different direction.

"No. No." The thug blocks her path. "Where do you think you're going?"

"Leave me alone!" She steps back. "What do you want?"

"You know what we want." He slaps his bat. "And I'll let you know if you've got enough of it for us to let you go."

Mary sees the headlights of an approaching taxi.

"Help! Help!" She frantically screams and runs as the gang chases. "Help me please!" She runs toward the vehicle, and a white male taxi driver slides a double-barrel shotgun out of the window. "Get away from her, you suckers, before I blow a hole in yo' chest!" The gang immediately scatters.

"Ma'am, it's okay now." He observes Mary trembling with fear. "You can come with me." He opens the back door, and she steps inside of the cab. "I can take you wherever you need to go." He drives away.

The driver sees Mary crying from the rearview mirror.

"Are you okay?" He stops the vehicle.

"Yeah." She wipes away her tears. "I'll be all right."

"I'm sorry for what happened back there."

"Thank you for your help."

"No problem. Where can I take you?"

"I need to go to Dominant City."

"I'm not allowed to go into that city, ma'am."

"I know. But can you get me as close as you can?"

"I can go to the employee's entrance at the back wall if that's okay?"

"Yeah, anywhere is fine."

"All right."

The streetlights illuminate a lifeless boulevard as the taxi travels toward a newly developed city in the far distance ahead.

Chapter 13

Dominant City

A host of hovering vehicles travel through an extravagant city of exquisitely crafted tall buildings.

A seamless, pearl white, super-stretch limousine with an elongated blacked-out windshield smoothly glides down an immaculate boulevard.

The limo parks near the curb of a unique skyscraper, and a white doorman approaches the side of the vehicle. He waves his hand and a carved outline section of a side window and door appears on the vehicle.

The entire carved section disappears, and several impressively dressed white men and women joyfully step out of the limo. The window and door section reappears and seamlessly integrates to the vehicle as the men and women proceed inside the building.

Fashionably dressed white people waltz to classical music as they meet and greet inside an elegant ballroom.

"So how's life for you now?" A senior white male tycoon standing near the dance floor converses with another senior of his equal.

"Not bad, considering America has lost a lot of money because of this big separation, of course."

"Odd, isn't it? I must say in all my years, I've never experienced such an extreme case of racial departure. But as always, I'm sure we'll benefit from our newly created environment."

"Oh, yes. As long as we stick together and properly utilize our resources, we will always maintain an elite level of distinct prominence with an opulent lifestyle. Don't you agree?"

"Most certainly. And I definitely forecast a blissful future for us all."

"Are you two going to stand here and talk all night?" A white woman wearing a beautiful evening gown approaches.

"Not at all, my dear," the tycoon says. "Shall we dance?" He extends a hand and escorts the lovely lady to the dance floor.

The headlights of the taxicab peer through the darkness as it travels along the beaten path of a narrow dirt road. The vehicle stops near a tall concrete wall. A gate with a blue force field blocks the entrance to Dominant city.

"All right, ma'am. This is as far as I can go."

"Okay, I'll get out here." Mary steps out of the taxicab and into the darkness.

"Ma'am, are you sure you're going to be okay out here by yourself?"

"I need to find a way to get inside this city. And I have no other choice."

"Okay, ma'am. I hope what you're doing is worth it."

"Yeah." She looks around the area.

"Well, be careful."

"Thanks." She closes the rear door, and he slowly drives away.

Mary notices a computer screen and a magnetic strip card reader mounted inside the wall near the gate. She touches the screen, and an automated voice responds.

"Welcome to Dominant City. Please insert an access card." She touches the screen repeatedly, and the automated voice continues, "Please insert an access card. Please insert an access card." She aggressively hurls a rock and cracks the screen. "Malfunction! Malfunction! Please enter your annual income and wait for security," the automated voice responds.

Mary sees the headlights of an approaching vehicle and quickly hides behind a tree.

A catering service van stops near the gate, and a white female steps out of the vehicle. She swipes a card through the magnetic strip reader, and the force field gate disappears while Mary discreetly enters the rear of the vehicle.

The van continues along the dark pathway and down into the mouth of a dimly lit tunnel. The van parks near other conventional service vehicles inside a parking lot.

The female caterer exits the van and walks through a service door for employees.

Mary steps out of the rear of the van, now wearing a waitress's uniform. She scampers through the service door and runs inside an open elevator.

The elevator doors close, and it ascends to another level. The doors reopen to an industrial kitchen, and Mary sees several white people cooking and preparing food. She proceeds through the kitchen and stands at the entrance of the luxurious dining room, where she sees white waiters and waitresses catering to very affluent white people seated at numbered tables.

"Come on. Don't just stand there." A female waitress quickly approaches Mary. "Here. Take this out to table number four." The waitress gives Mary one of two food trays. "Hurry!" She quickly moves on.

Mary walks past table number four and places the tray on table number ten in front of Kathy Goldstein, a lovely and mature white woman with silver gray hair sitting among her peers.

"What are you doing?" Kathy scowls at the food. "I didn't

order this! Take it away!" She looks up, instantly recognizing the waitress. "Well, well, if it isn't my half-black sister, Mary."

"Hello, Kathy. I was hoping I could find you."

"And why would you be looking for me?"

"Well, I was hoping to see my sister and maybe become friends again."

"Hmmm … let me see. Your black husband left. You're broke, and now you need your real family back. Is that right, Mary?"

"I see you're still stuck on skin color! I married him because I love him!"

"Well, it's obvious he didn't feel the same way about you."

"That's what's wrong with this world now! Eddy was my choice, and he should've been welcomed into my family!"

"You don't get it, do you, Mary? Your husband and everybody left because they wanted to be with their own kind. So I'm here with my own kind, and everybody's happy."

"You must be crazy if you think this separation hasn't affected us all!"

People seated nearby become very attentive to their conversation.

"Excuse me, my lady." A white male host rushes to Kathy's side. "Would you like to have this truculent insubordinate expelled?"

"No, I'll deal with her for now."

"Don't worry. I'm leaving!" Mary steps back. "You think because you sit behind a big wall with your so-call friends that you're safe from the destruction of this planet? Well, you're wrong. Because hate has no skin color."

"Okay, I've heard enough. Now it's time for you to go."

"This world will never change with narcissistic racist people who think like you!"

"I said leave!" Kathy stands up. "Now!"

"Yeah, okay. One day I hope that you can see we're all in this together and you're no better than anyone else." Mary walks away.

Chapter 14

A small militia group of Arabic men swiftly drive jeeps and trucks over a Middle Eastern desert.

"Stop here," the militia leader instructs the driver of the jeep as he points to a designated location in the sand.

The leader exits the vehicle with a small briefcase as the other men gather closely.

"Thanks to our new ally, our time has now come!" He opens the briefcase and shows an embedded handprint scanner to the men. "We must strike down the feeble nation of separation!" He places the briefcase in the sand and inserts his hand on the scanner. "We will show them how strong we have become!"

The handprint glows bright red and a tripod of large missiles emerge from the ground.

"Death to America!" the leader exclaims in his native language as he looks to the sky and frowns.

The powerful missiles begin to rumble and shake the earth as they take flight, inspiring the men to cheer.

US Intelligence Command Center

White male and female military personnel keep diligent watch over several computer surveillance monitors. A computer screen abruptly flashes an image of three incoming missiles and sounds the alarm.

A white male defense chief sees the words "Intercept Immediately" on a second monitor.

"Get me the president!" Then the president appears on a very large computer screen. "What's the emergency?"

"Mr. President, we have three very hot missiles coming in from the Middle East, sir."

"What's their target?"

"They're approaching New York, and we don't have much time, sir."

"Execute the Liberty."

"Yes, sir."

The Statue of Liberty eyes glow bright red and her torch begins to vigorously spin and open. A small missile is fired from the torch, and she turns to a different direction. She partially lowers her arm, and a second missile is fired. She turns again and fires a third missile.

The defense chief observes the monitors as they display a digital image of all three US missiles approaching the enemy missiles. Two US missiles intercept and destroy two enemy missiles, and the computer image disappears.

The third US missile flies directly into the path of the last enemy missile. The warhead of the enemy missile sprouts wings and ejects just before the two missiles collide.

All indications of missile activity disappear from the command center computer screens and the officers celebrate with sighs of relief.

"Good job, you all," the president congratulates.

"Thank you, sir."

Moments later the computer screens flashes an image of the incoming warhead and sounds the alarm.

"What is it? Are there more missiles coming?" the president inquires.

"No, sir." The chief inspects the monitor. "It appears that the enemy missile has divided and its warhead has just breached our airspace, sir."

"Where is it going?"

"I'm not sure. It's possible that we may have thrown it off target, sir."

The warhead screeches across the sky of a big city and flies over an American flag high on top of a tall building as the command center continues to track the approaching image.

A white female pulls the arm on a slot machine, and three cylinders inside the device begin to spin. As each cylinders stop, the words "Lucky" "You" "Win" align across the front of the slot machine.

"I won! I won!" The gambler becomes highly exuberant in the midst of onlookers as the machine begins to blink and whistle. "Now I can live behind the wall with the rich people!" She dances, and the casino instantly explodes.

Emergency lights shine through the smoke-filled wreckage as the bloody and injured exit the building and make their way into total mayhem on the flooded boulevard.

Several white male and female protesters holding "unfair labor" and "unfair government" signs chant as they parade in front of the US White House.

"Good morning, Mr. President." The defense chief enters the president's office and salutes.

"Good morning." The president observes the protestors from a window behind his desk. "Give me an update." He looks at devastating pictures of the Hoover Dam and flooded Las Vegas.

"The report's not good, sir. As you can see, the dam is completely destroyed and most of the state of Nevada is flooded, sir."

"Damn it!" He strikes his desk. "Who could have done this?"

"Sir, there are also incoming reports of a greater concern."

"And what's that?"

"Well ... because of our decline in population, other nations have considered us weak and may be conspiring to take over this country, sir."

"Okay, who do we need to send a message to?"

"Unofficially, I believe this attack may have been orchestrated by another source operating from another planet, sir."

The president ponders this information and again looks over the pictures of destruction.

"I need you to step out of the office for a moment please."

"Yes, sir." The defense chief salutes and immediately walks out of the office.

The president removes a wireless keyboard from a drawer and places it on top of his desk. He types a sequence of letters and numbers, and a spectrum of light emanates from the top of the keyboard.

The light begins to create an image of Zordyn Kenyapha wearing a black leather ZKC uniform with a gold-colored V-shaped pattern and collar.

"Mr. President, why is my presence being requested?"

"You know damn well why I called you!" The president

stands and moves in front of the image. "Do you see the hurt and damage you've caused to innocent people?"

"Total race separation, isn't that what you people always wanted? Or, are you accusing me for this segregated war started by your ancestors centuries ago?"

"I see you are a very deceiving man, Mr. Zordyn. And I also see anger and confusion as a weak point of your leadership."

"No! Don't blame me for the inevitable destruction of Earth, when surely the white man has negatively influenced every race on the planet! But not anymore, you won't!" Zordyn steps forward. "Now that the black man has finally come to power."

"I'm not afraid of you!" The president stands face-to-face with Zordyn. "If war is what you desire, then war is what you shall have."

"No, not me. But the great separation will bring destruction upon your land."

"No. It sounds to me like you're prophesying toward your own demise."

"You see a lot for a man who's going to lose everything. I need not waste any more time with you." Zordyn steps back. "From now on, all communications with Earth will be severed. And as far as I am concerned, blacks and whites will never stand together peacefully again." The image of Zordyn fades away.

Chapter 15

Graffiti that says, "Stop Black-on-Black Crime," "Hate Follows Anywhere," and, "No Justice, No Peace," is written everywhere on the streets of the urban community.

Many very light-complexioned black people smash windows, loot, and set fires as they protest in the neighborhood.

Several dark-complexioned police officers violently spray the uncontrollable civilians with water cannons. Other officers unleash doglike beasts, allowing the four-legged animals to aggressively attack whiter rioters as they wrestle insubordinates to the ground and put them in handcuffs.

Under the cover of darkness, a small group of black men wearing hoodies discreetly rush inside a narrow opening on the side of a crater. Torches are mounted on walls and light the way as the men move forward inside the cave.

The small group joins a variety of light-to-dark-complexioned black men surrounding the recruiter, a medium-complexioned black man standing on a platform.

"Welcome, brothers." The recruiter notices the small group

of men. "I ask that you all please remove your cover." The people remove their hoods, and Bobby, Eddy, and Geno are among them. "Thank you, gentlemen," he says and then continues, "It was a big mistake for all of us to follow Zordyn Kenyapha. We now see running from our problems on Earth has led us to the same problems here on Mars. There are no magical words or profound statements I can give you to unmask discrimination or further describe the destruction of racism that has not already been discussed. You must understand that hate will continue to follow us wherever we go. So until we individually decide to change in our minds and in our hearts, the only thing you'll keep changing is your location."

The crowd applauds.

"We must put an end to this evil injustice everywhere! I'm not an African, African-American, or Martian! I'm a man, a human being! And I'm proud to be among you other black men!" He looks over his audience.

"I still believe all people can peacefully live together if we try hard enough. So I'm going back to Earth by any means necessary! Now who's with me?"

The crowd applauds again.

"Good, because I have a plan." A small round device opens in the palm of his hand and shows a tall building. "This is the executive building where several armed men will be in position and ready to strike Zordyn's ground security. The rest of us will be headed to his top-floor office." He displays the progression of the plan on the image.

"Zordyn's not there!" Bobby steps forward.

"Who are you, brother?"

"My name is Bobby Walker, and I was one of his executives."

"Please come forward."

Bobby moves closer.

"What can you tell us?"

"Zordyn would be expecting someone to come looking for him on the top floor, but his office is on the thirteenth floor."

"Thank you for that information, my brother." The recruiter nods. "We're all in this together. Is your group with us?"

"Yes, we are!" Eddy steps forward.

"Very good."

The recruiter again looks over all the men. "Now then, by a show of arms, are you all ready to continue to fight for what's right?"

The crowd cheers and waves their laser assault rifles in the air.

Four dark-complexioned male security officers dressed in black body armor stand guard with assault rifles on the steps of the ZKC executive building.

A group of black men wearing hoodies and armor-plated vest discreetly approach the security officers from below.

"Stop!" The first officer sees one of the hooded men creeping up the steps.

The man begins to shoot quick bursts of red laser beams at the officer as he quickly moves up the steps. The officer double taps his left shoulder, and a blue layer covers his body armor, deflecting the multiple shots.

"I can't get him!" The man shouts to another hooded man as the officer shoots quick bursts of laser beams at them.

"You gotta shoot 'em in the head!" the other hooded man shouts to the men.

The other three officers activate their blue body armor and also begin shooting laser beams at the hooded men.

The first officer's laser blasts the hooded man in his chest, killing him instantly, but a second hooded man sneaks up the steps and shoots the officer in the back of his head.

Another officer shoots the second hooded man in his back while other officers repeatedly blast holes in the steps, sending several more hooded men screaming in the air.

After an intense laser battle, many hooded men lay dead on the steps, and the three security officers are killed as more hooded men proceed to the building's entrance.

A light-complexioned male rebel sees the fourth security officer crawling away, bleeding from head wounds.

"Open the door!" The rebel removes his hood and places a gun barrel to the officer's face.

The officer struggles to reach the glass entrance and dies. The rebel places the officer's hand on the bottom of the door. The officer's palm is scanned, and the door unlocks.

The rebel quickly runs inside the building with a group of hooded men.

Eddy, Bobby, the recruiter, the rebel, and a group of hooded black men all position themselves outside a large office door on the thirteenth floor.

Zordyn sits on the edge of a steel-plated desk with his arms wrapped around Teakena.

"Congratulations." She kisses his forehead. "You've accomplished what no man has ever done before. Thanks to you, we now have a beautiful city with such an appropriate name, "All. To. Zor-Dyn." She looks into his eyes. "So what's next?" She slides her hands down the front of his uniform.

A huge explosion knocks the office door off its hinges, and several hooded men rush inside, shooting laser beams at Zordyn.

Teakena is shot in the back, and Zordyn leaps behind the desk as she falls to the floor. Two gun handles extend to Zordyn from the rear of the desk, and four gun barrels poke through holes in the front of the desk as red laser beams bounce off the steel plates on the desk.

Bobby and Eddy quickly jump to opposite sides of the office as Zordyn begins to violently shoot yellow laser beams from all four barrels. The yellow lasers slice through the walls, brutally killing the recruiter, the rebel, and all the hooded men as they enter the office.

Zordyn pushes a red button underneath the desk and quickly straps himself inside his chair as a portion of the floor begins to slides open.

"He's trying to get away!" Bobby announces as the chair begins to descend.

Eddy quickly slides his rifle underneath Zordyn's desk, and it gets caught between the bottom of the chair and the top of the floor.

Zordyn unstraps himself and tries to remove the rifle. Eddy quickly jumps on his back, and they fall to the floor in an intense battle.

Zordyn positions himself on top of Eddy, strangling him.

"Stop!" Bobby shoots Zordyn in the back, and he falls off of Eddy.

"You fools will never destroy my empire!" Zordyn frowns as he lies on the floor.

"Your empire!" Eddy stands over him. "Who do you think you are? God?" He kicks him.

"Those who were first on Earth shall be last on Mars!" Zordyn grabs Eddy's leg. "You're black, and you should never turn your back on family!"

"You're right. That's why I'm going back to Earth." He breaks free of his grasp. "And I'm taking whoever wants to go back with me!"

"You wanna leave?" Zordyn opens his hand, revealing a small triangular device. "Then let's all leave together." He tosses the device to the center of the floor and laughs as it begins to blink and unfold.

"Come on! Let's go!" Bobby dislodges the rifle and straps himself inside the chair as it descends.

Eddy slides over the desk and grabs a hold of the chair as it begins to rapidly move down a shaft.

Zordyn stands in agonizing pain and runs toward a large glass window. He double-taps his left shoulder just before impact, and two small wings extend from the back of his uniform as he free-falls out of the window.

A massive explosion blows out the thirteenth-floor windows as Bobby and Eddy run away from the building.

"Wow!" Bobby stops and looks back. "I guess that's it for Zordyn."

"I won't miss him."

They continue to witness the destruction.

"Do you still remember that last password you used?"

"Yeah, think so. Why?"

"Aren't you ready to call Mary and tell everybody we're coming back?"

"Yeah, I've been ready to do that for a while."

"Well, ain't nothin' stopping you now."

"Let's go!"

They continue to run away.

Chapter 16

A large metallic saucer-shaped spaceship slowly passes over Dominant City and its surrounding wall near the US White House. The white citizens of the affluent community cease all personal activity, bringing the city to an abrupt standstill as they all gaze upon the passing vessel. The less fortunate, poorly dressed whites aimlessly walking the streets of Baltimore all stop and stare at the spaceship as it passes over the run-down city.

"Come on. Let's see where it's going!" a less fortunate white female pedestrian says and then motions to a group of locals standing in the street.

The spaceship flies over a neglected football stadium and extends three legs as it lands on a parking lot in front of a huge crowd of white people.

Whites gather around the spacecraft as the top separates from the bottom. The bottom compartment is completely filled with a diverse crowd of black people as it lowers to the ground.

All the blacks and whites stare at one another in silence as Bobby and Eddy emerge from behind the onlookers.

"You see her?" Eddy asks as they search from the spaceship.

"Nah, there are way too many people out there."

"We've got to find her."

Mary pushes her way forward, keeping watch of the spaceship as she moves to the front of the crowd.

"There she is!" Bobby points.

"Mary!" Eddy yells and waves.

Mary locates Eddy, and they immediately start running toward each other. And as if an alarm had sounded, all the people urgently start running toward one another with cheers of great joy.

"Oh, Mary, it's so good to hold you again." They tightly embrace. "Please forgive me for leaving."

"I wasn't sure I'd ever see you again." She begins to cry.

"I'm sorry." He wipes away her tears. "But I told you I was coming back, didn't I?"

"Uh-huh."

"Oh, Mary. You're so beautiful." He kisses her face.

"Hi, Mrs. Haze." Bobby steps forward.

"Hi, Bobby." She extents her arms. "I'm so glad to see you guys again."

"Me too."

They cordially hug.

"May I be a part of this celebration?" Mary turns around and sees Kathy standing behind her.

"Yes! Yes, of course!" Mary and Kathy hug each other. "You remember Eddy, don't you?"

"Hello, brother-in-law."

"Hi, Kathy. It's good to see you."

"Yes, and I need to apologize to both of you. Mary, you were right about what you said, and I also got a chance to see the world without color." She looks at Eddy. "And it wasn't very pretty. She extends a hand toward Eddy. "I was wrong." She smiles.

"Well ... the future of Mars didn't look too bright either." He pulls Kathy and Mary closer, and they pleasantly embrace.

"Kathy, I want you to meet Bobby Walker." Mary pulls him closer.

"Hi, Ms. Kathy."

"Hello, Bobby."

"He's one of my old students."

"Oh, okay. It's a pleasure to meet you, sir."

"It's nice meeting you."

They shake hands.

"It's amazing to see everybody coming together." Mary looks up and sees another spaceship passing over the city.

"Yeah." Eddy looks up. "And I promise to never leave you again."

"Till death do us part, remember?"

"That's right. I love you, Mary."

"I love you too." They passionately kiss as blacks and whites meet one another throughout the parking lot.

The US White House sits picture-perfect on a beautiful sunny day. The US president is broadcast on all television screens world-wide as he sits behind his desk and speaks.

"A question was once asked years ago. And that question was this: Can we all just get along? Unfortunately, the world responded negatively. I have been forced to realize that a nation divided cannot stand and that no man or race can live to his or her fullest potential without the help of someone else. Prejudice, racism, and discrimination will destroy us all wherever we go. I also have a better understanding that all people are unique and different in their own ways. That is why as president of the United States I am pleased to have all people return to Earth and reclaim citizenship of this nation. We must take advantage of this new opportunity to start an open and equal relationship with all people. This is the only way America can ever be great for all of us. United, we stand, and this is my pledge to all people. I hope you all will join me. Thanks for listening."

The seamless, pearl-white, super-stretch limousine with the blacked-out windshield smoothly glides down the same spotless boulevard.

The limo parks near the curb of the unique skyscraper, and the white male doorman approaches the side of the vehicle. He waves his hand, and a carved outline section of a side window and door appears on the vehicle.

The door section disappears, and Mary, Eddy, and Kathy exit the vehicle with a racially diverse group of men and women.

A blue ZKC Excel glides alongside the limo. The doorman approaches the vehicle as Bobby and Jessica step out.

"Hey, guys! Wait up!" Bobby shouts to Eddy and Mary. "Don't scratch my paint." He tosses the remote control to the doorman.

Mary, Eddy, Bobby, Jessica, and Kathy all happily move and groove along with a variety of other people dancing to the live music inside the elegant ballroom.

Love and hate can be viewed through the eyes of good and evil.
How do you see the future?

Printed in the United States
By Bookmasters